A LITTLE DESTINY

Also by Vera and Bill Cleaver

Vera and Bill Cleaver

A LITTLE DESTINY

LOTHROP, LEE & SHEPARD BOOKS
New York

First Edition   1   2   3   4   5   6   7   8   9   10

Library of Congress Cataloging in Publication Data
Cleaver, Vera.
   A little destiny.
   SUMMARY: Doubting that her father's death was purely accidental, 14-
year-old Lucy and her family confront destitution and a formidable adversary
in their small town.
   [1. Death—Fiction. 2. Family Life—Fiction] I. Cleaver, Bill, joint author.
II. Title.
PZ7.C57926Li   [Fic]   79-10322
ISBN 0-688-41904-6   ISBN 0-688-51904-0 lib. bdg.

A LITTLE DESTINY

Chapter One

At noon on the day Papa was taken from us, the sky was a fretwork of dark slate blue and Mama, at her needlepoint in her upstairs sitting room, said she believed it would snow.

Sure enough along about two o'clock the cold crystals began to fall, and by three p.m. the scene from our parlor window was bleached. In the kitchen a roasting duck spit its oven juices, and Delia went from room to room replenishing the fires. Never the servant, though that is what she and her husband Marion were in the house of Commander, she moved with authority, drawing the velvet window coverings, setting a bottle of claret and a glass on the table beside Papa's chair, placing his slippers on the hearth. In my inglenook I turned the pages of my book. What joy! My tutor, who came every day save Saturday and Sunday, was ill. The world had calm and depth. Why not, in a world so abundant and comfortably arranged?

The clock struck four and the clock struck five and Papa and Marion did not return and did not return from their day in the country, where Papa was holding one of his auctions. The snow stopped and commenced again and Mama came down the stairs, pausing on the last one for there was a commotion at the front door. I went to open it and in stepped Mr. Thomas Clegg and then Marion. Papa was not with them and I think it was I who asked where he was.

Mr. Clegg formed his answer. He wore a greatcoat and all of it was buttoned from hem to neck, and I saw the dull red stains on its sleeves and front and saw that his gloves and the toes of his boots were smeared, too. He held out one of his hands to me and said, "Lucy." And then turned to face Mama and said, "Annette."

"Tom!" exclaimed Mama. "What is it? What is wrong? Where is Earl?"

"There has been an accident," said Mr. Clegg, unshrinking. "I think we had better all sit down."

"Yes," agreed Mama. "Let's all sit down." But she continued to stand where she was and so did I, in the way people do when they know before being told that some horror has befallen. The flames in the fireplace sent their sparks up into the chimney. Marion came out from behind Mr. Clegg and his face was terrible. He was crying. As he started past Mama, she stepped in front of him and said, "Marion, where is Mr. Commander?"

"At the undertaker's," gasped Marion, and fled to the comfort of the kitchen and Delia.

And so Mama and I received the news of Papa's grotesque death from Tom Clegg. A moneylender born to the grovel fields of Georgia but risen above them, he was known in private circles as one who put his money out at high interest rates in various ways. He maintained offices in one of the more modest business sections of Church Falls and his home, though it lacked the grace and nobility of age, was one of the town's finest. Throughout the county he was admired and respected for his business abilities. A widower, he and Tom Junior, who was my age, had been dinner guests in our home many times. We and they were members of the same church. In his philosophy Papa, in particular, had always regarded Tom Clegg as one of his friends.

He was not that and soon we would know it. First, though, there was this, the ripping sound of Mr. Clegg's voice rising, falling, flooding, taking. It did not falter. "We were out at the Whidden farm," he said. "Whidden had been wanting to auction off some of his cattle for a long time and Earl was there to do it. I was there because I have an interest in the Whidden place. I wish I hadn't gone. Annette, I couldn't save him. I couldn't!"

"Go on," said Mama.

"There was a yearling," said Mr. Clegg, "and Earl tried to drive it into a holding pen, but it ran from him and jumped into a dirt bank, and Earl went after it and leaped astride its back. It jerked up its head and one of its horns about two or three inches long penetrated Earl's jugular vein."

I said, "His jugular vein," and Mr. Clegg's head began to weave like that of a charmed snake's, and my own was filled with fluid that rushed and then drained, and then I was on the floor and Mr. Clegg was bent over me. I looked up into the dark, unconsoling holes of his eyes and, in that lost and immense moment, it was as if I saw him running around inside himself. He was fleeing from something and he was lost, too, but he was laughing. It was as if he had some kind of queer sickness. I wondered if ever again I would have the strength to speak.

Mama was calling to Delia and Marion, "Come! Come quickly!" And when they did and tried to help me, I pushed them away and stood and reeled toward Mr. Clegg crying, "Liar! It's a lie! Take it back!"

Marion came after me. His arms went around me, holding me. And Mr. Clegg, accepting Mama's apology for my behavior, said, "It's understandable. She is but a child fourteen. The minister and some of the ladies from the church will be here soon. If I can be of any service to you, Annette, you know you have only to so notify me."

"Yes," said Mama. "Yes."

Mr. Clegg pulled the collar of his coat up around his neck, went to the door, and let himself out into the snowy air.

Dinner was unthinkable. Mama sent Marion to the telegraph office carrying a message to be sent to my brother Lyman, a newly established doctor of medicine at College Springs, a town one hundred miles to our southeast. Our minister and some of the ladies from our church arrived and, after a little hushed visit and some prayer, took Mama with them to the undertaker's to make arrangements for Papa's burial.

I slipped away from Delia and, without a coat or any

other kind of wrap, went outside and walked around the house twice, keeping to the shadows. The coldness and the darkness, so unphysical, quieted me. I went to the cabin at the rear of our house that was home to Delia and Marion, and I knelt at its stoop. A dovecote containing Marion's pet pigeons was there and I pushed its covering branches aside, opened its latticed door, and put my hand inside and touched one of the warm birds. I brought it out and held it, feeling the beat of its heart, and my own expanded and finally I wept.

Marion found me there. He took the bird from me and lifted me, and I leaned against him. "Papa always liked the pigeons."

"I know," said Marion.

"And the snow. You remember that time all of us walked from here to Jewel Sink in the snow? It took us all night and we didn't do anything when we got there except build a fire and eat icicles. Papa wanted me to see how muskrats lived, so when it got to be day again we all went down to the spring and he punched a hole in the ice. We saw one swimming around but he wanted to come up for air and was afraid of us, so we only watched for a second. Papa said the water was theirs first and ours second. Do you remember that?"

"I remember," said Marion.

"Papa always had different ideas and he didn't care if people laughed at them. He laughed, too. He liked a good time. He liked the fun in people."

"Yes, he did."

"But I was his love. He always said so. Did you send the message to Lyman?"

"I sent it."

"Where is Delia?"

"She's cleaning up."

"Is Mama back?"

"Not yet."

"Lyman will come, won't he?"

"He'll come."

"He will have to be the head of our house now."

"That's right."

"Marion, did you see it when it happened?"

Answered Marion, "I saw it." There was a secrecy in his voice, a scar. In the dovecote the pigeons made their sleeping noises. Marion had put me away from him. I could not see his face.

"Marion?"

"Miss Lucy, I don't want to talk about it now."

"I do. Mr. Clegg didn't tell it all and I need to know it."

"Miss Lucy, he told it all."

"No, he didn't. He held part of it back. There was more to it. I saw. I know. You must tell me, Marion. You *must*. You owe it to me."

As we count the years Marion was still fairly young and strong, but then he was an old man and the day had weakened him and so, as one met with something he could not handle alone, he told me.

14

In the dovecote the drowsing pigeons talked to each other. Marion broke a switch from one of the bushes beside his stoop and without vigor whipped the air with it and said, "It was like Mr. Clegg told it, except when the yearling turned on your daddy I jumped into the pen, too, and run toward him, but Mr. Clegg grabbed up a shovel and came at me. He was yelling like silly and wouldn't let me past him or go around him. Miss Lucy, this is ugly. You shouldn't be wanting to hear it."

"I want to hear it, Marion. Every word."

I could hear Marion swallowing and swallowing. He threw his switch away and stood with his arms hanging and said, "Well, so then I hollered to Mr. Clegg that I needed to get to Mr. Commander and try and help him. He was on the ground and he was bleedin' bad, but he wasn't dead. Mr. Clegg wouldn't let me help him. He hit me on the back with his shovel and run me out of the pen. He tried to play like he didn't know what he was doing, but he did."

"Where was Mr. Whidden?"

"Him and his hands had gone back up to the big house to drink coffee."

"So no one saw what actually happened except you and Mr. Clegg."

"That's right. Afterward he told the rest of them, but he didn't tell it right. He told them I was scared and had run out of the pen."

"And they believed him?"

"They believed him. Mr. Clegg is who he is and I'm who I am, so they believed him. Miss Lucy?"

"Is that all of it, Marion?"

"That's all of it. Except then Mr. Whidden and Mr. Clegg and one of Mr. Whidden's men put your daddy in Mr. Clegg's car and then started back to town."

"Was Papa dead then?"

"No. He died on the way."

"Did he say anything before he died?"

"I don't know. I wasn't with the others. I was driving Mr. Commander's car. I was following."

"Why, Marion?"

As if I had struck him, Marion stepped backward. "Why was I driving your daddy's car?"

"That isn't what I meant and you know it! I meant why did Mr. Clegg hit you with a shovel and run you out of the pen? Why wouldn't he let you go to Papa's aid? *Why did Mr. Clegg want Papa dead, Marion?*"

"I might could be wrong," said Marion, after a moment. "It was a long time ago."

"What was?"

"A long time ago," said Marion, "Mr. Clegg wanted to marry your mama, but she already had her sights set on your papa. He was dynamitin' stumps then and doing anything else he could get ahold of to make a dollar."

"Did you know him then?"

"Not good. Delia and me had just come here from South Carolina, and we was eatin' lard on our bread ourselves, and taking any kind of work we could get. When we was out of work we'd go fishin' and one morning, when we was out on the river trying our luck, we saw Mr. Clegg

16

come out of the bushes about twenty feet from where we was. He had so many chains wrapped around him, it was all he could do to clank down to the water and wade in. It only took us a minute to figure out what he was up to. He never did thank us for saving his life. Right then Delia said he never would and she was right. About a year after that, your mama married your papa and Mr. Clegg married, too. His wife was a Summerhill and they said she was ten years older than him. The Summerhills had money, but they all had something wrong with them and died early."

I said, "Oh, Marion, all of that sounds so crazy. It makes my head hurt."

A stream of air passed between us and, tenderly, Marion said, "I had to tell Delia about what happened this morning but what we think is, we shouldn't tell your mama and Lyman and neither should you."

"Marion, what are you saying? Of course I'm going to tell them. Of course I am. It's their right to know just as it was mine."

"In politics and other ways Mr. Clegg is a powerful man," said Marion.

I said, "That may be, but I still can't keep this to myself."

"No," agreed Marion, "I reckon you can't." He left me then, and I sat there alone in the cold watching the rising smoke from one of our chimneys color the night and listening to the voices of the night whispering, *Lucy. Lucy.* I stared into the blackness and tried to think of Papa as being somewhere, but in spite of my scripture learnings could not think of him as being anywhere except nowhere. He was not with God. He was not up near the stars. He had not returned to any part of nature. He was simply gone, and his goneness produced in me a numbing and silent anger that was to remain silent and enjoin Marion and Delia to be silent, too. It would turn me, this anger, from the support of all my old ideas and dreams and what my culture had made of me, and I would become someone else.

First though, there was this period of in-between with none of us knowing quite who we were anymore or what it was we were supposed to do.

Some people have grand and queer notions about security. They think they can own it. That is not true. Security is not anything that anybody can possess. It is like a painter's or a musician's gift. Some of us are only allowed to use it for a while. Security is a slippery commodity.

Lyman did not respond to Mama's first message so, in the afternoon of the following day, Marion was sent to the telegraph office with another. This time there came a reply from the clerk in charge of the Western Union office at Lyman's town which read: "So far unable deliver your message. Much sickness roundabout here."

Mama received this news with agitation, but then her mother's patience exerted itself. She said, "Well, Lyman is a doctor and I can imagine not all of his patients are able to come to him. He is probably out in the country caring for a sick family. We shall simply have to proceed without him if necessary."

The day we put Papa to his final rest we still had

had no word from Lyman. There was a stillness over the spent cornland and the brown pasturage around the cemetery. To its north, about twelve miles distant from the limits of Church Falls, there was our property at Jewel Sink, an inherited, uninhabited place of great hemlocks and red oaks and a relic of a house which my grandparents Commander had once called home. There was a cluster of outbuildings and a good water supply provided by Jewel Springs, but we had never used this property for anything save a picnic ground. We drank the water from the deep spring without qualm.

On this day, standing with Mama and Marion and Delia at Papa's gravesite, I thought of all the good times we had had at Jewel Sink. The sun was dim and distant, and in the air there was the smack of winter. In a nearby field children, taking a shortcut from school to home, paused to watch. They swung their lunch pails and speculated behind the backs of their hands. One of them, a child with long, bright hair, callously gnawed away at an apple, and I was reminded of my own younger self and thought of the good teachings and endeavors of Papa.

Mama did not want the grief of friends or associates nor did I, so that evening she and I sat in her upstairs sitting room. After we had talked awhile, she brought the black metal box containing Papa's legal papers and documents of ownership to her writing desk. After a search of her memory, she recalled that Papa had always carried the combination to its lock in his watch case.

We got the box open and what did we find? We found

19

that we did not own our home nor much of anything in it. Even our automobile, which was generally regarded as one of the more superior models of the time, was mortgaged to Mr. Thomas Clegg. There was a sheaf of notes covering the mortgages—all of them, according to their "call" dates, past due.

Mama viewed the papers spread out before us and hid her downcast eyes with one fine hand. Her voice shook when she said that the papers were old ones and that she was confident the reason they had not been destroyed or otherwise disposed of was only an oversight on Papa's part. By Marion she sent a note to Mr. Clegg asking him to come at once. Mama was the only child of parents long deceased, and I had never seen her pluck a chicken or sweep a room or transact any business except when dealing with door-to-door peddlers. Papa had always been her provider and protector. I had always viewed her as that kind of person who largely lacked self.

Mr. Clegg did not lack self. That evening when he had come in response to Mama's invitation and after he had sampled a pony of Papa's choicest brandy, he moved from his chair to Mama's writing desk and began to examine the documents in question. He and I only exchanged brief greetings, and during the concern of his examination he kept glancing toward the settle on which I was seated forward with my elbows on my knees and my feet flat on the floor.

Papa would have gone about this business in a relaxed manner, for he had owned that kind of disposition. He could have been a pie maker or a field peasant and still have been a whole person, not overly sensitive to the world. He had not been driven through life. He had been able to laugh at it and shut it out and go his free way. He had not loved himself but had been able to accept himself.

Mr. Clegg was a lesser creation than Papa. His research was something to watch. When he had finished, he raised his head and to Mama said, "I am afraid what you have here is the truth. I have been so busy with other affairs I had forgotten, but there is no mistake. As you can see, these have all been legally recorded and they have not been satisfied." He was making a pile of the documents and restoring them to their box.

Mama had risen to face the moneylender. Her pale hair was loose around her face, and she stood slim and erect. "I thought Earl might have made some kind of private settlement with you. That is why I asked you to come. He never told me that he was in debt to you."

"There was no private settlement," said Mr. Clegg. The light from the lamp shining on him showed us the gleam of white at his throat and wrists. He had a Roman nose and his lips were smooth and delicate like a woman's.

"Then what this means," said Mama, "is that we have been living beyond our means for a long time, and now it appears that we are bankrupt."

Mr. Clegg was preparing to go. Pontifically, he said, "Annette, you have had a cruel day. I don't think we should discuss this anymore tonight. It looks like more snow, and I want to get home to my own fire, and I think you should be resting. There is no great urgency here. We will work out something."

"No great urgency," said Mama, with her hands clasped.

"No urgency at all," said Mr. Clegg, and Marion, quiet as a ghost, came to show our visitor out. Going down the stairs, our departing guest held himself aloof and Marion kept his own distance. At the foot of the stairs Delia waited with Mr. Clegg's coat, hat, and muffler, and he took these from her gravely.

From a high window I watched the figure of the money-lender leave our yard and close the gate behind him. There was snow shine and star shine and I watched him go to his car. He turned and looked back. I could not see his face. He was not a large man and there was nothing about him that suggested evil, yet I knew that I was looking at evil and before I let the velvet drape fall back into place I spoke a promise: "Clegg, I am going to get you."

No one heard.

Chapter Two

There are these particulars to be noted, all connected and all pushing us toward that time when each of us would find out what kind of selves we were, how the world and our outside dealings with others had shaped us, what kind of material lay in us.

Lyman arrived the day following Papa's funeral. He was wayworn from his journey and said all he wanted to do was lie down and sleep the clock around, yet he did not go to his old room and bed. For an hour he and Mama talked in her sitting room. Then he came and found me and asked me to drive to the cemetery with him, saying he wanted to see Papa's grave. Mama had given him Papa's watch.

I said, "I don't feel like going to the cemetery again. It's hideous."

Lyman took an irritated turn around the room and came back to me. "Lucy, you have to stop crying. Papa would be ashamed of you to see you hiding in here like this."

"I'm not hiding. I'm just being alone."

"You are hiding and it's not good for you. Have you eaten anything today?"

"No. I don't want to eat. What I want won't come from our kitchen."

"Lucy," said Lyman, showing me his fatigued eyes. "Papa is gone and nothing can bring him back."

"You don't know how rotten it is. It's rotten, rotten."

"Of course it is, but there is nothing to be done about it. It was an accident."

"I'm sick. Go away."

"I want you to go to the cemetery with me," said Lyman. "Here's your coat. Get up and put it on. And put something warm on your head. This is flu weather. College Springs is crawling with it and it's traveling this way. Will you at least drink a glass of milk before we go?"

"No. And if we go to the cemetery, we'll walk. Otherwise I'll stay here and you may go alone. I won't ride in the car."

Lyman gave me a look and said, "I pity the man you will someday marry. You are childish and spoiled and you keep your mind closed to others. Our car is the same one it's always been."

"It isn't ours. It belongs to Tom Clegg and it smells now just like he smells. I hate him."

"You hate Tom Clegg? Why?"

"I hate him."

"Because we are in debt to him? Lucy, that doesn't make sense. Haven't you ever heard of business? What do you expect Mr. Clegg to do? Just hand everything over to us? He can't do that. He is a business man."

"He is a fiend," I said.

Lyman would not continue the argument. He did not

look like a doctor twenty-eight years old, but more like a boy grown to adulthood too fast. His feet and hands were small like Mama's, his guileless temper imitated her, too.

But we walked to the cemetery and during the walk passed one of Church Falls' more ornate houses. It was Greek-columned in front and its wide verandas and door trim displayed extravagant iron work. An iron picket fence guarded it and its grounds. Lyman, saying he felt bleary of a sudden, paused and rested a hand on one of its spikes. The sky had height. Said Lyman. "Lucy, Mama and I have decided what we must do."

I said, "I heard. Next time don't make me eavesdrop or else choose a room with a bigger keyhole to do your talking in. My ear is still numb."

The hills in the whole surround were bronze-colored and Lyman pushed himself away from the fence. At the cemetery we stood, one on each side of the stone that marked Papa's grave. Lyman did not cry, nor did I. We did not speak. There was nothing left to speak about. The plans were made.

Lyman would go to see Mr. Clegg and make arrangements to liquidate the notes held by him. There would be no trouble with this. Mr. Clegg was a friendly and reasonable man.

Lyman would then go back to College Springs, close his practice there, and return to Church Falls to work.

Delia and Marion would find other places of employment.

My tutor would be dismissed and for the balance of that school year I would study at home under Mama's direction.

We would learn to be prudent, living with less but still in decency and comfort and dignity.

I had heard it all once and now on the way back from the cemetery I heard it again. Lyman wanted to know if I disagreed with any of it and I said, "No." Because that was all I could give him, he was so serious and anxious and dutiful and there was Mama waiting at our gate for us.

By one of his footboys Mr. Clegg had sent a container of live oysters, packed in salt-watered straw and ice, along with a letter to Mama assuring her of his sympathy and friendship and telling her that he would be out of town for a few days, but would see her when he returned.

Delia cooked and served the oysters for our dinner that night. The portion on my plate was a punishment and afterward, in the kitchen, Delia said, "Well, you fooled your mama and brother, hiding these in your biscuit and pie, but you can't fool me."

I said, "I notice you didn't eat any. I would have just as soon tried to swallow brickbats. Have Lyman and Mama talked with you yet about what we are going to do?"

"We've been notified about it," answered Delia, hanging her dish towels to dry.

"How can you be so calm?"

"I'm not calm. What you see is not what is."

"It's so hateful. I don't see why we can't at least tell

Lyman the truth about what happened out at Whidden's farm."

"Don't you?"

"What do you think he'd do?"

"I can't picture that, Lucy."

"Do you think he would go after Mr. Clegg?"

"Probably."

"And kill him?"

"I think he would try."

"And then what?"

"And then," said Delia, "he might go to prison." Her face, her lady's face, offered a frail and accomplished smile, accomplished because it said everything and said nothing. Delia was afraid, not only for Mama and Lyman and me but for herself and Marion as well.

Lyman spent only thirty-six hours with us before taking the train back to College Springs. He said he could wait no longer for Mr. Clegg's return and instead penned and left in Mama's care a letter proposing a system of installment payments which would satisfy the mortgages held by Mr. Clegg.

For his farewell meal Delia cooked Lyman his favorite dishes. He ate little and admitted to feeling punk. Delia had cleaned and pressed his clothes and, when the time came for the temporary good-byes, she told him, 'Well, you're wearing the big shoes now. How do they feel?"

"They're a little loose," confessed Lyman.

"You'll grow into them," said Delia. "You are not to

27

worry about your mama and Lucy. Marion and I will be here looking after them."

"But I told you we can no longer pay you," protested Lyman. "You must go. You won't have any trouble finding another place. Everybody in Church Falls knows you."

"We will stay on till you get back," said Delia and, as if Lyman were a child again, yanked his woolen cap down over his ears.

The weather had faired off. We who lived above the state's fall line felt the faint warmth of the sun again.

We settled down into a day-to-day waiting pattern. There were changes. In mourning, Mama received no callers. Delia did not overload our table at mealtimes. I counted and recounted what money I owned and delayed buying the school tablets I needed. My tutor was dismissed and I, scarcely able to keep my mind on my textbooks, studied alone. From every page Tom Clegg looked out at me. I could not drive his phantom image away. I saw him in many postures and predicaments, all commanded by and obedient to me. In a hunter's trap surrounded by snarling, gorging beasts. In a field running before the lash of an oxhide whip. On his knees before me with his neck bared to my knife, pleading for his life while it left his frantic flesh in a red stream.

Mama graded my study papers and did not voice her dismay. That was left to Delia, who said, "You're worrying your mama and ought to stop it. Even I could write a better composition than this."

I said, "Leave my papers alone. They're mine and this is my room."

"You and Lyman are all she's got left now," said Delia. "You had better be thinking about that. Your future is her future and how is it going to be? You think Lyman can do it all?"

"He's a man," I said. "And he's the head of our house now."

Delia lifted one of the sheets from my study table and gazed at it long. "What is this, a new language?"

"It's art."

"A man without a head is art?"

"I buried his head behind the church door."

"I'll be glad when Lyman gets back and takes over here," said Delia. "You scare me." She tore the sheet lengthwise and then crosswise and fed the shreds to the fire.

We waited for Lyman, waited for some apprising word from him, and waited in vain. Mama wrote to him and sent him telegrams, and her trouble and expense gained us nothing.

Came Mr. Clegg late one evening. Handsomely dressed and eager as a young lover, he bore a gift of hothouse flowers. He said that he had only returned to Church Falls that afternoon. Mama asked him to join her in her sitting room, and I watched him, nimble as a boy, take the stairs two by two. Delia and Marion had gone to one of their church meetings.

This was a night of significance. The house was still

29

and most of it dark. The doors all were locked, the velvet drapes drawn. There was no danger, nothing to fear, not in the sense of bodily fear.

In my reading corner beneath the stairwell, I felt fear and twice left my nook and went up the stairs and stood on the landing listening. I heard the voices behind the closed door running on, and then stopping, and then running again. The keyhole was a rejected temptation. I raised the courage to go forward and tap. Immediately the door opened and Mama, with cheeks too pink, but aristocratic and regal as a queen, said, "Oh, Lucy. Mr. Clegg was just leaving."

The flowers Mr. Clegg had brought were on the floor. They looked as if they had been thrown there and Mr. Clegg was shooting his cuffs, making a thing of showing composure. He had not a look or a word for me. In a contained and civil enough manner, he said to Mama, "Thirty days, Annette."

Mama had swung the door wider. "Good night, Mr. Clegg. Lucy will show you out."

"Thank you," returned Mr. Clegg. "I can find my own way." He said, "You have pride, Madam, and it's admirable, but now I think you will see it in the dust." He came through the threshold and went past me and down the stairs, setting his feet precisely on each one.

I entered the room and looked at Mama on her knees gathering the discarded flowers, and I went to her and took the long-stemmed blossoms from her. The moisture in them hissed as the flames in the grate consumed them and Mama, with tears in her eyes, laughed. "Oh, Lucy, it was so funny.

Can you imagine at my age and his? He asked me to marry him. He tried to kiss me. He said he could make me forget your father."

"How did you answer him?"

"I couldn't. Even if Tom and I were both young again and I had never been married to your father, Tom wouldn't interest me. The things that matter most to me he has never seen and never will but I couldn't tell him that. He wouldn't have understood. I laughed at him. I couldn't help myself, it was so ridiculous and clumsy. So awful. So funny."

"It is not funny, Mama. What did Mr. Clegg mean when he said thirty days?"

"He meant," replied Mama, "that we would either pay him within thirty days or walk away from here leaving everything on which he holds a lien."

"Everything on which he holds a lien. Mama, how do we *know* that Mr. Clegg holds liens on anything of ours?"

"Oh, Lucy," said Mama. "I've been over that a thousand times in my mind. Naturally it has occurred to me that Tom Clegg might be lying. Naturally it has, but there is nothing on our side to confirm that. Your father was always careless in his record-keeping and with his money. In a way, though it causes us to be troubled now, that's one of the reasons I loved him. Money wasn't your father's life. Oh, I *wish* we could hear something from Lyman. Why on earth doesn't he let us know something?"

I said, "I don't know. Maybe you ought to let Marion take the car and drive to College Springs. Have you thought of that?"

"Yes," answered Mama. "But as it stands the car is not ours. If Marion should have an accident on the way, that would only create more trouble with Mr. Clegg. Marion is not so expert behind the wheel as your father always encouraged him to believe. No, we'll wait. Surely in a day or two we will hear something from your brother."

I said, "Mama."

And she looked at me, my little lady, a wife without a husband. Was she also a mother without children? In an hour, two hours, she would go to her bed in the great house and alone face emptiness. Why were not her children, Lyman and I, doing for her? She had seated herself and taken up her needlework and said, "What is it, Lucy? Did you want to tell me something?"

"No," I said. "I've forgotten what I was going to say. Move closer to the fire, why don't you?"

Sleep time in our house, so still it was. During one of its deepest hours, I made a decision and rose and made my preparations. A note to Mama pinned to my pillow, a valise packed with two changes of clothing. In the chill and the silence I sat, cloaked and hatted, waiting for the first streaks of dawn.

There was an early train which would take me from Church Falls to College Springs. When it pulled out of its station I was in one of its coaches. It was unheated and, across the aisle from me, three other passengers sat hugging themselves. I thought they must be a family. The little boy wedged between the man and the woman looked to be around eight or nine years old. He had an untamed look in

32

his eyes and was a twitcher. No part of him was still for over five seconds at a time. The father, seeing me shivering, heaved his bulk from his seat, came across, and obligingly closed my open window. He asked me if riding on trains made me sick, and I said no. He said he and his wife always got trainsick, but that little Willard, their son, never did.

It was not long before I found out for myself about Willard. He was a real firebrand as he rushed from one end of our coach to the other, leaping over the feet of the other passengers, as he played Ride 'Em Cowboy from the high backs of the vacant seats, as he sprang back into the aisle and did Indian war whoop dances, as he twirled and flung his arms wide and roared and waddled, pretending to be a bear. I thought he must be one of those children that come to some parents in middle life. His supply of energy was endless. Soon he was purple in the face and panting for breath, but still did not stop his sport, except every now and then he would pause for a second and look around at his back end as if questioning whether it was keeping up with the rest of him.

By this time we were out into the open country and rolling along at a pretty good clip, although the roadbed under our wheels must have been faulty for there was quite a bit of lurching and swaying taking place. Willard's mother and father had arranged themselves in their seats so that they were half sitting and half reclining. They had their mouths and their eyes clamped shut and, with every lurch and sway, little moans escaped them.

Willard continued to have himself a fine time. He

passed my seat on the run just as we went around a rather sharp curve. This motion caused the mother and father to be thrown against each other and their eyes flew open. In a small panic the mother pushed herself erect, looked around for Willard and, spotting him in the act of pretending to be having a seizure of some kind for the benefit of two bonnetted ladies, fell back again against her seat. "Say something to the boy," she implored her husband. "For heaven's sake, speak to him." Willard's tongue was hanging from his mouth and he was staggering around.

The father raised himself up, opened his eyes, and after a couple of tries got them focused on Willard. In a weak and trembling voice he called out, "Howdy Willie."

Before our train reached College Springs, Willard and I got to be friends of a sort. He told me he had a buddy named Desperate Dan. I said, "What is he desperate about?"

Willard thought long before he confessed, "I do not know. I do not know what desperate means."

I said, "Well, I don't feel like explaining it to you but, if you want to know how it looks, look at me."

Willie said one time he grew a white potato weighing four pounds and none of it hollow either. I had an afghan with me and would have enjoyed settling down under its warmth for a little snooze, but each time I tried Willard would lean over me and pry one of my lids open with a thumb and forefinger and start another of his self-history stories. "I used to be a diving champion."

"Oh, I knew you were not an ordinary person."

"Until they made me quit it."

34

"Why?"

"They thought I might get to be famous and rich and then somebody would kidnap me."

"And they did not want that to happen?"

"No. I'm their onliest child. Last year I was health king at my school. You ever seen anybody as healthy as me?"

"Right at the moment I can't say I have."

"I drink me a pint of pot liquor every day."

"Ughful."

"The best kind is what comes from mustard greens."

"Ughful."

"You want a peppermint?"

"No, thanks."

"Want to play some Scotch-Hopper?"

"I think I can forego it."

"You talk funny. Where you from?"

"France."

"Where's that at?"

"Around the corner and under the tree."

Willard let my eyelid drop back into place and gamboled back to the far end of our coach to pester the two bonnetted ladies until we reached College Springs.

As I viewed it from the platform of the train station, this town did not appear to me to be a triumph over anything. Its air was free of soot, though, and the streets looked wide enough to permit the passing of two vehicles. I looked around for a public conveyance but did not see one. Also, there seemed to be a lack of people.

The train, still with Willard and his parents aboard,

pulled out and I went back inside the station and asked the agent if it was a town holiday. He answered, "No. The reason it looks that way is because most everybody is home sick."

"With what?"

"The influenza. Pneumonia. Pleurisy. We got a regular epidemic going on and no doctor. What is it you might be needing from me?"

I said, "I am Doctor Lyman Commander's sister. Can you direct me either to his home or his office?"

"They are one and the same," informed the agent. "But he is down, too. You got your brother's good looks. Is that one piece here the whole of your baggage?"

"Yes. Can you direct me to Doctor Commander's place?"

The agent came out from behind his counter. We walked outside and he pointed. "Through that little park there and then a right turn. You won't miss it. The house is green and there is a sign in one of the front windows. Tell your brother I said hey and I hope he gets better before the epidemic gets worse."

A few minutes later I set my eyes on Ryder Tuttle for the first time. He was sitting in what I took to be Lyman's waiting room with his nose buried in one of those fictionalized cheap magazines which tell about murders and outlaws. There was a fire going in the freestanding stove in the center of the room, and Ryder was sitting behind Lyman's desk with his booted feet propped up on one corner of it. The place looked and smelled as if it had not been cleaned or aired for a month of Sundays.

My entrance did not take the immediate interest of the man behind my brother's desk. He looked up and said, "The doc is sick and can't see nobody but, if you owe him and are here to pay, I am authorized to take your money and draw you a receipt."

I said, "I am Doctor Commander's sister. Who are you?"

"I am Ryder Tuttle," came the reply. The magazine was laid aside, the feet were removed from the desk. I now received great attention.

I said, "Where is my brother?"

"He is upstairs asleep in his bed where he ought to be," replied Ryder. "I thought you might be another one of them soup ladies is the reason I didn't get up when you came in. I know they mean good, but they are beginning to rub my nerves. They always want to talk to me about my sins."

"Are you my brother's assistant?"

"Hooroar," said Ryder. "No, I am afraid you cannot class me as anything proud as that. Due to circumstances beyond my control, I am a trunk peddler at the present time. It is a terrible way to eke out a living. Having to cater to cookie ladies and all them Sunday school types."

"Sunday school never hurt anybody."

"They always want everything guaranteed. I tell them I don't make my pins and needles and scissors, I only sell them, but they don't believe me. So the next time I stop at their house, I got to look at anything that is rusted or busted and make it good, even if it is a month later. And on top of that, if the little woman of the house is a widder or something like that, I got to sit with her for two hours and hear all her troubles. Last year I bet I ate fifty pounds of cookies while hearing all them women's troubles. Looking at me, can you believe I never used to measure but about twenty-nine inches around my middle, including my belt? Look at this belly I got on me now. Forty inches at least, and I cannot walk it off. I walk ten to fifteen miles a day with a trunk strapped on my back. Wouldn't you think that would shrink this pot some? It don't. I am going to get out of the trunk-peddling business as soon as I can get these boils on the back of my neck fixed up. The doc said he would take care of them for me just as soon as he got well enough to hold a knife again. If I had me some good old Denver Mud, that would draw them to a head, but I see the doc don't keep any on hand. Maybe it has gone out of style. The man at the drugstore didn't know what I was talking about when I tried to buy a can of it off him."

I said, "How long have you been here?"

"I think a little over two weeks," answered Ryder. "You don't happen to be a nurse do you?"

"No. You think you have been here a little over two weeks? Doing what?"

"Taking care of the doc's business. Mostly that has just been sitting here telling people who come in that he is sick. I have taken in a few dollars that was due him. I have been sitting here getting caught up on my reading and trying to think of a different way for myself. If there was a war going on anywhere, I would go fight in it. Maybe, now you are here and I don't have to worry about the doc being left here by hisself, I can get myself together and ease on. He has been awful sick and is still not out of the woods. The day I walked in here, he was passed out clean on the floor over there. I carried him up to his bed and, when he came to, that is when he hired me."

"Have you received any telegrams for Doctor Commander?"

"Two. They are here someplace."

"Why did you not reply to them? My mother sent them to my brother because she has been worried about him. A telegram usually means urgent business of some kind, don't you know that? You must be an irresponsible person."

"Halloo!" exclaimed Ryder. "Now that is no way for you to talk to me, girl. I have been doing the best I can here with what I have to work with. I have not been studying no telegrams. At the time they came, things was in kind of a hurry around here. They still are. Last week eight people in this town died from the flu."

I said, "I will go up and see my brother now."

"He is not in any condition to do much talking," said Ryder. "He don't need to talk. What he needs is to put something in his stomach besides snail water and soup. The ladies of this town do not know how to make good soup. Mostly it is cabbage and H-2-O. Sometimes they let a little grease walk through it."

39

"We will talk about food and other conditions when I come back down," I said. "While I am gone, you could air this room, and don't put your feet on the desk anymore. It is scarred enough."

Ryder sent me an amused look, but got up and went to the door and opened it, and the fresh air came sailing in.

I could have wept to see Lyman lying so pallid and wasted, hunched under four blankets in his lumpy, stingy bed. His forehead was warm to my touch and he talked a little. He inquired after Mama and Delia and Marion and told me he was on his way to recovery, and he said he had been reasonably successful in collecting the monies due him from those patients he had treated since being in College Springs. He told me there was another doctor coming to take his place in the town and asked if Ryder Tuttle was still downstairs but, before I could answer that one, he was asleep again.

I returned to the downstairs and saw that Ryder had his hat on his head and was preparing to leave. He had set his upended trunk just inside the closed door to the waiting room. A hip-length coat was draped over one end of it. It was lined with sheepskin and the cuff to one of its sleeves was missing. There was a neat row of currency laid out on Lyman's desk. Ryder was sitting behind it with his feet on the floor and his face again stuck in his trashy magazine. "They have taken to lying in these things," he observed. "A leopard don't run off into the bushes and change his spots because all of a sudden the milk of human kindness starts running in his veins. If I am not a authority on anything else I am one on that. How is doc feeling?"

"He is finished here," I said. "He is sick and I do not see how he is going to get better lying up there in that wretched room. There is a new doctor coming to take over for him. This building is like an icebox."

"Well, your brother has only been renting it, and the owner of it died last week along with them other seven I told you about, so wouldn't be much standing in your way if you wanted to take him home with you soon as he is able to travel. Me, I am going to be on the next outbound train. I think there is one passes through here about eleven o'clock tonight. I have decided these boils won't kill me, but the flu might. If you decide to chance it and stay here with your brother till he is on his feet again, there is plenty of firewood out back. I sharpened the doc's axe yesterday so it might pay you to handle it with some respect."

"I have never handled an axe in my life," I said.

"Oh," said Ryder, "just don't let your feet or your hands get in the way of its blade and you will make out all right. There is not much to wood chopping." Poetically, he said, "I do not like good-byes so never say any. I just say adios. If fortune will have it, we might meet again on life's road someday."

That silly and senseless statement made me impatient. I said, "I don't know what kind of arrangement you had with my brother for your services but, if he owes you, you may take some of the money there on the desk, or you could

41

leave me an address where you might be reached, and I will ask Mama to send you what my brother owes you as soon as I get back to Church Falls. I have nothing against good-byes so I will say mine to you now. Good-bye. Good luck."

Ryder stood and walked to his trunk and lifted his coat. From one of its inside pockets he withdrew a large flat bottle, unscrewed its cap and took a long swig of its amber-colored liquid. He appeared to be considering within himself. "I had me a hot bath when I first got here and I been sleeping in a nice warm bed. The menu hasn't been what you would call A-1 but, as you can see, I have not starved to death so I figure the doc and me are level. So you will not be needing my next address. Anyway I am just fresh out of one."

I said, "What is that you are drinking?"

"It is vanilla," answered Ryder. "It has alcohol in it and is warming. Do not worry, I am not taking anything that does not belong to me. This is from my own private stock. I always keep me a few bottles on hand. It is good company when I am out on the road on cold nights. It is cheaper than whiskey and, besides, I was never much of a liquor drinker. Is there anything I can do for you before I go? I mean anything that will not take over five minutes."

"It would take me that long to tell you what you could do for me," I said. "So no, thank you. I will manage. And as I said before, good-bye."

Ryder had another pull at his bottle. "All your brother has had to eat today is some hasty pudding, Tuttle style. What he didn't eat I put back in the kettle on the stove.

It has lost some of its looks since morning but, if one of the soup ladies does not show up again pretty soon, I would heat up what is left if I was you and give her another try."

I said, "Do not worry about us."

"If I was you and decided to clear out of here, I would do it all at once. A town in trouble like this one is fair game to thieves, so don't leave anything behind and expect it to be here when you come back for it. You maybe could get the agent at the railroad station to help you. He owns a dray and a team of horses and, I believe, would loan them to you. If I am not getting my people mixed up, he still owes your brother for amputating one of his little toes. He dropped a sadiron on it when he was a little kid, and it grew back crooked."

"Do you think I could get him to come and pack Lyman's equipment and all this other stuff for shipping?"

"I doubt it. He has a job to tend to."

"I have never driven a team of horses."

"There is not anything to that. Dray horses only know one thing. How to pick them up and set them down. They never heard about racing for a living. You just point them in the direction you want to go, and tell them when you are ready, and they take you."

"Well, I shall manage. Lyman will be my biggest concern. I think he is too weak to walk even from here to the railroad station. I suppose after I get everything loaded I could fix up a pallet on the dray for him. How much do you suppose that desk there weighs?"

A deep pink flush was spreading through Ryder's

cheeks, creeping toward his nose and forehead. In a remonstrant tone, he said, "Well, hooeee. You make it sound like I am ditching you. Girl, I am not ditching you. The last time I ditched a female she deserved it and I do not know you that good."

"Nor will you."

"We are only two boats that have passed in the night."

"Ships."

"Boats. Ships. They are all the same to me. I do not like either. One time when I was still green I went to sea, but it did not work out as I had it planned. The first chance I got, I jumped ship." Ryder seated himself on his trunk. The vanilla was getting to him. Every minute or so he would treat himself to another tipple from his bottle. "I say I do not like ships or boats neither one. Give me the good old terra firma. Give me the blessings of good old Mama earth. We understand each other. I have not always been anything so low and ignorant as a trunk peddler. You would not believe the story of my life. What do you think of a mother and a father who would run their only child off when he was ten?"

"I would have to think a minute to answer that."

"Well, that is what happened to me. They gave me a dollar and told me to hit the door. I confess I was not exactly no sunbeam to them, but they wasn't one to me either. I was smarter than they were for one thing. They could never see bad fortune as their friend, but I could. It and me has always been bedfellows. It is a good teacher. When you see it as your master, it will do it every time."

"Do what?"

"Take you to fields of glory," said Ryder. He got to his feet and went past me to Lyman's patient-examining room. I heard him open a drawer. In a minute, he returned bearing a lancet. He asked me if I knew what it was and I told him I did.

We made then what Ryder said was a lopsided deal. It was in my favor he said. I would lance his boils for him, and then dress them as Lyman would have, and in exchange for this service he would not only assist me in getting Lyman and all his personal belongings and professional equipment back to Church Falls, but would travel with us.

I said, "But I have never lanced anything before."

"Well," wheedled Ryder, "it might be a tickler business, but it is my neck, not yours. The only thing is, what comes out of the boils once you get them opened up might give you the whoompses. If you feel one coming on, holler quick and I will jump out of your way."

We did not get Lyman, all of his personal possessions and professional gear, and ourselves out of College Springs until three days later. Ryder did not have the habit of hurry and was not so expert at getting things done as I had believed he would be, yet he was willing and cheerful and I could not have managed without him. I sent Mama two wires, the first telling her that Lyman was alive but ill, and the second telling her when to expect us and to send Marion to meet our train.

Once we were aboard the train for Church Falls, the conductor arranged two seats opposite mine and Ryder's so that they formed a small bed, and Lyman slept all the way.

Ryder did not shut up for more than five minutes at a time during the whole trip. Taking care to keep his voice low so as not to disturb Lyman, he talked as if he had been deprived of human conversation for a year. Ninety-nine percent of his jabbering concerned himself. "I am tired of being a trunk peddler."

"So I gathered, three days ago."

"There is no future to it. I have got a little coin laid back in the old kick and think, when we get to Church Falls, I will hole up somewhere and have a look around for something with a little destiny to it. A big, strong man like me ought to be at something with some fashion. What do you work at?"

"Don't be silly."

"That's silly?"

"I don't work at anything."

"Why?"

"Because I don't have to. My father has always taken care of me."

"What does he do?"

"He is dead now. He was killed recently."

"How?"

"By a yearling. Papa jumped on its back and it turned on him and one of its horns penetrated his jugular vein."

"That is a peculiar way for a farmer to die."

"Papa was not a farmer. He was an auctioneer."

"I worked on a ranch one time."

"Where was this?"

"Colorado."

"Did you like it?"

"I liked it better than I like being a trunk peddler. I am a good mechanic with tools and livestock. By heart I guess my calling is to be a dirt farmer. I would be out there in Colorado yet but I have never been one to back out of consequences."

"What kind of consequences?"

"All kinds. There is always somebody standing around with a head full of consequences, and he has got the draw on you because you don't have any. The reason you don't is because he has got nothing you want, but you have got something he wants. So you are just lying there thinking about Saturday night and the good time you are going to have with it when it gets there and you can go to town, when in he comes and starts throwing his consequences at you."

"He comes in where?"

"In this particular case it was a bunkhouse."

"And what is that?"

"You are not much up on things are you?"

"I am up on my own kind of things."

"A bunkhouse is a building where cowboys and ranch-hands live."

"You said there was a man of consequences. What was it you had that he didn't?"

"Well," said Ryder, "that was the funny part. I never found out. He was the foreman and was living good, better than me or any of the other hands. He liked to skin people,

47

especially them that didn't speak his lingo. He tried it on my little Mex pard, and I called him on it, and that is when him and me went a few rounds. I did not want to fight him but I did. Beat him, too. He had a touch of the outlaw in him and went for his gun, so I had to do a pretty good job on him. Then me and my little Mex pard got out of there pronto. It was not the best of time in the year for it. There was snow in the passes and sometimes we would have to detour."

"Have you mentioned your little Mex pard to me before now?"

"He was a runt and a nuisance, too. He didn't speak but about five words of English, so usually I had to do most of his work and let him take the credit for doing it. I was sure glad to say adios to that one. We parted company as soon as we got down close to the Mexican line."

The train was pulling into the Church Falls' station. I woke Lyman and told him we were home. Faithful Marion was there to meet us. He helped Lyman to our car and then came back to help me with the hand luggage. We left Lyman's crated equipment at the station for future pickup.

I thought Ryder was glad to take leave of us. At the last minute, again I offered him some of Lyman's precious dollars. He gave my offer his interest for a second but then shook his head. He was busy with his trunk and, as soon as he had it on his back, asked me where he could find cheap food and lodging, and I recommended the Packard Hotel. "It is a hotel in name only. Actually it is a boarding and rooming house. Mrs. Packard used to come and help our regular servants whenever Papa gave one of his big parties. She is plain and simple, but pleasant and honest. You may tell her that you know Doctor Commander and me and she will take you in if she has a vacancy."

Ryder thanked me for the medical attention to his boils. He tipped his hat and set off down the street whistling and swaggering.

Marion had put Lyman in the back seat of the car and had covered him with a blanket. During the drive home, I asked Marion if Mama was all right and he replied, "Yes, she is all right. While you were gone she found Delia and me another place, so we will be leaving you all the tail end of this week."

Those last days with Marion and Delia still with us sped around. Helpless and afraid and loaded down with the secret we shared, I watched them dismantle their home and carry the packed boxes to the waiting car. I wanted them to say something wise to me, to leave me something of themselves to draw upon, but seeing them, uprooted and adrift and wronged themselves and submissive to being so, I turned away.

Chapter Three

Almost as much as I missed Marion and Delia, I missed Marion's pigeons. They had always had so much to say as they flashed around the house, as they wobbled through the grasses bobbing their heads and showing their affections for one another.

We lived during this time on the money Lyman had brought with him from College Springs and on the food-stuffs in our pantry and cellar. Delia had always been skillful at hoarding dried and preserved foods.

One of the easiest accomplishments in life is to rid yourself of friends when they want to be rid of you. They came and, seeing our changed lives, came no more. Lyman slammed the door on the backs of the last of them. He lived, I thought, on fantasies while the precious days went and came and went again, each drawing us closer to Clegg's deadline.

Now convalesced, Lyman went out and attempted to sell the land at Jewel Sink. And returned bearing defeat. He tried to borrow money from banks and found out that his standing in the community was more than a league away. He made paper plans to turn three of the downstairs rooms into professional ones and hired two burly men to haul his equipment from the train depot and set it in the rooms he had chosen for his practice. They worked with the surliness of the underpaid, but by duskfall he had his waiting and examining rooms and office. He placed his physician's sign in one of the front windows.

The patients did not come. There were already too many reputable, established doctors in Church Falls. All Lyman's seniors, they courteously invited him to their luncheons and dinners, and he did attend one of their evening affairs, but only Doctor Porter was big brother to him. That old tacky practitioner was regarded as third-rate by the more fashionable physicians and the better people of the town. He wore a white moustache, stained yellow by tobacco and coffee use, his combination home-office was on a back, unpaved, and unlighted street, and his patients were farmhands, domestics, and the "hello girls" who entertained the errant males of Church Falls.

It was Doctor Porter's reputation that he preferred drinking to working and, one morning while Mama, Lyman, and I were still at the table, he came and made an offer. Would Lyman be interested in becoming his associate?

Lyman set his cup in his saucer. Now at last his defenses, all of them, had been taken down and here, undignifying and unflattering though it was, was opportunity. So he became Doctor Porter's live-in partner, and Mama and I went to live in two rooms at the Packard Hotel, one for sleeping and the other for all purpose. The sleeping one had no built-in closet but was furnished with a cedar-lined wardrobe that stood in a corner on four legs. We would share a community bathroom with six other second-floor guests. Cooking in the rooms was not allowed. There was a boarding house dining room on the main floor where meals were served at conventional hours.

Mama satisfied Mrs. Packard's curiosity by looking her straight in the eye and saying, "My husband and I made some bad investments just before he died, so now Lucy and Lyman and I must make a new way for ourselves. Lyman has living quarters at Doctor Porter's, so the arrangements I am making now do not include him. These rooms will only be for Lucy and me."

Mrs. Parker's plain face grew some embarrassed color. I asked her if Ryder Tuttle was one of her lodgers and she answered, "Why, yes. His room is on the first floor."

I asked, "Is he working at anything?"

"I believe," said Mrs. Packard, "he is working as a rent collector, but I am not positive about that. So long as they behave themselves and pay on time, I make it a point not to meddle in the private lives of my guests."

There was a sign on the back of our door which gave us permission to bathe either between the hours of ten and eleven in the mornings or three and four in the afternoons. This grant amused Mama. I told her I did not think it was a bit comical, and she said, "Your father would have thought so. When we were first married we lived in a room like this."

One of the worst features of our living at the Packard was idleness. Our rooms, dressed out as they were with Mama's personal possessions and mine, required but little attention to keep them neat, and after that there was nothing to do but study, do needlepoint, read, and wait for lunch and dinner. The other lodgers showed no inclination to mix with us. Out of thralldom of habit or whatever else drove their appetites for doing nothing, they spent many of their hours on the hotel's porches.

Mr. Clegg was seldom out of my mind.

When his schedule allowed the time, Lyman came and took his meals with us. The woman who served our table was Oriental and wore an ankle-length dress of linsey-woolsey, hitched up in the front with a piece of twine. I asked her where Ryder Tuttle kept himself, and she said he left the hotel early every morning and did not return till late at night and that he took his meals elsewhere.

Lyman rebuked me for asking after Ryder, for in those days he was still class-conscious. In Doctor Porter's horse and buggy outfit he drove around town and out into the country making calls on the sick. He worked long hours and his income was sorry and a source of friction to him; it provided only food and shelter for Mama and me, yet he would have it no other way. Without his knowledge, Mama sought employment in the millinery and dressmaking shops. Her search was unsuccessful. I suggested that I go out looking for some kind of work and she slammed her hairbrush down on the dresser. "You are a child, my child. And as long as I have any authority over you you will do as I say. You will not go out looking for work. You will apply yourself to your studies."

For lack of other evening entertainment, Mama and

I took long walks and one night went as far over as the Commander house and saw that it had turned Clegg. The night was dun-colored, and we stood under a tree on the opposite side of the street, and the minutes we stood there seemed like hours. To my eyes, the house we viewed was not the same as when we had lived in it. The drapes in its foremost rooms were not drawn and I could see that it was as it was when Papa was alive. To the beautiful tapestry that hung above the fireplace, the plush chairs, the cut-glass decanter standing on Papa's little leisure table, all of the room's former elegance was there, and yet something that had been grafted into it when it was Commander seemed missing now that it was Clegg.

In her throat Mama sighed, and we moved away from the tree, and walked again. I looked back to see the cabin where Delia and Marion had spent so many contented years. Its muddled shape was a disturbance and I thought, We don't belong to ourselves anymore. We don't know where we are going.

The night was a vast emptiness. I felt its chill in the roots of my hair and I thought, Somebody has to make something happen. The thought came and once it had come it would not stand still. It did not come alone. There was another: It is I who must. There was a thick noise in my ears.

When we got back to the hotel, Mama went upstairs at once saying she wanted bed and sleep. I found Ryder Tuttle in the far corner of the empty lobby reading one of his trashy magazines. On the table before him there was a composition book, such as the kind schoolchildren use, and several stubs of pencils.

I went over to Ryder and sat down in the chair nearest him, and he looked over at me and said, "Well, halloo there, Chief. I was wondering when I was going to bump into you again. Mrs. Packard told me you and your mama was living here now, and that your brother had gone into business with another doctor. How is the world treating you?"

I said, "Oh, I am uptown now and wonder why I didn't come before. I see your reading tastes have not improved."

Ryder glanced at the magazine in his hand. Its cover proclaimed that it contained "another great and true story by Scotty Bloodheart." Said Ryder, "Well, I was not presented with no education like some people I know. Old Scotty here knows how to spiel a yarn and that is all that matters to me. The only thing about Scotty is, he is not always right in his particulars. I been studying his stories, and I have come to the opinion he has not ever seen a man hanged. A man on the wrong end of the rope don't always die on the instant. Sometimes it takes him twenty or thirty minutes to jerk hisself to death."

"Have you ever seen anybody hanged?"

Ryder pulled his composition book toward him and took up one of his pencil stubs. "Not more than a couple of times."

"Did it bother you?"

55

"No. They deserved it. In fact, hanging was too good for them. Had I been their judge, they would have been part wolf by now."

"How is that?"

"I would have fed them to the wolves. Maybe while you are just sitting there doing nothing you would be so kind as to tell me what portend means."

"When you portend something you predict it."

"I wished I knew about words. I would give a pretty if I did. Then I would go old Scotty one better. Did you know people get paid for writing stories?"

"I have heard rumors to that effect. If that is your ambition, you should not be wasting your time on Scotty Bloodheart."

"Who should I be wasting it on?"

"Herman Melville comes to my mind for one."

"Never heard of him." Ryder gazed at me, licked the end of his pencil stub, and wrote a word in his composition book. "Scotty Bloodheart is partial to having people portend. In every one of his stories he has somebody portend at least four times. I will not be a copycat. I will say that they predict."

"In what?"

"In a story I am going to write as soon as I get all the words collected and straight in my mind. Help me think of a new name for myself. I do not want anything fancy like Bloodheart."

"Are you serious?"

"Why would I not be?"

"People who write stories are usually educated. You said yourself a minute ago that you wished you knew about words, and that's an admission that you don't. How are you going to get past that obstacle?"

"I have not figured that part out yet. I will deal with it when I come to it. Probably I can find somebody to school me."

"I do not think that will be an easy matter. How old are you?"

"Eighty-six. I do not look it though, do I?"

"Mrs. Packard said you were working as a rent collector now. Is that more to your liking than being a trunk peddler?"

"I was a rent collector up till about two hours ago. Now I have joined the pack of the unemployed."

"What went wrong?"

"Chief," said Ryder, "I was not cut out for that job. Threatening poor people to either divvy up or get out is not a honorable way to make a living. There is too much meanness in the world. I have been thinking I might become a bartender. I would make a good one since I do not believe in partaking of alcoholic spirits myself, except a little vanilla now and then for pain and loneliness."

"If you become a bartender, will you stay on here at the Packard?"

"I guess I will. I got no place else to go."

"Do you think bartending and living here in this hotel is your destiny?"

"What?"

"A few days ago you told me you were looking for something with a little destiny to it. Do you think bartending and living here is it?"

"No, Chief, I don't. But I do not see anything better rolling uphill to meet me. Have you ever seen a stagecoach running around a mountain with two wheels hanging off the road?"

"No. I have never seen a stagecoach."

"Neither have I, so I think I will not make the mistake old Scotty here does and try telling about them. Have you thought of a new name for me yet?"

"Not yet. Do you think if you did see your destiny rolling uphill to meet you you would recognize it?"

Said Ryder, "They ain't anything wrong with my eyesight. One time I rode in a posse out in Texas, and I shot a man's little finger off at twenty paces."

"What had he done?"

"He was a horse thief and had taken part in lynching a innocent man. I do not believe in thieving or lynching."

"What do you believe in?"

Ryder looked around as if he might see his beliefs hiding in one of the lobby's corners. He leaned and from his satchel beside his chair brought forth a little, greasy paper sack and opened it. It contained fried chicken hearts, but that is not what he called them. He called them thumper gizzards and said they were left over from his supper. He did not offer to share them with me and talked with his mouth full. He said he believed in God and his country, but added that his faith in persons was a little on the question side.

I said, "If you believe in your country then you have to believe in persons. The country would not be a country if it did not have persons in it."

"I have met but a few persons I would care to take up with in a permanent way," objected Ryder. "You look at it your way and I'll look at it mine. When I said I believed in country maybe I should have said empty country."

"How do you feel about muskrats?"

"They're cute little fellows. Smart. There isn't anything prettier or sweeter than an empty space of country when the sun is coming up or going down, especially if it is yours and there is nobody hanging around watching every little move you make, just waiting for you to make the wrong one so they can tell you to haul buggy on down the road. That happened to me one time."

"What was the reason?"

"I tore up a field," explained Ryder. "I didn't know how to use a plowshare then. The man who owned it is still green in my mind. He was one mean porker. One day when I first went to work for him I saw him beat one of his mules near to death. I used to think about going back there and killing him. He would not pay me my final wages. I was only fifteen then."

"If you had gone back there and killed him, how would you have done it?"

"I believe a gun would have been the weapon of my

choice. A gun is clean and quick, and they do not fizzle on you if they are in the right condition and you know how to use them." Ryder had finished his thumper gizzards. He said he was thirsty for water but not just any old kind. "Where I was this afternoon they had a deep well, and one of the little tykes pumped some for me, and I drank about a gallon. If I had had me a jug, I would have brought back some."

I said, "I know the taste of well water. We own property at Jewel Sink which my father inherited from my grandparents Commander, and there is a deep well on it. When Papa was alive we used to go out there and picnic in the spring and summertime. We have never used the property out there for anything else because Papa was not a land man, and neither is Lyman. Lyman has tried to sell it but was told that it is useless."

Ryder's face, surmounted by his thick crop of reddish hair, registered a protest. "I was to Jewel Sink one time when I was a trunk peddler. Spent the night there. It might have been your house I slept in. There wasn't any no trespassing signs, so I just helped myself. I had to sleep on the floor. I remember the owls kept me awake." With one of his pencil stubs Ryder drew a child's version of a cat with a curled tail in his composition book. "I did not see anything wrong with the land out there. I have never seen any that was not good for something. I wished I owned me just a little piece."

I said, "If you did, what would you do with it?"

"If it had a house on it," replied Ryder, drawing

another cat, "I would fix it up. I would do that first so I could live in it. Then I would make a study of the property and find out how to make it support me."

"Ryder," I said, "do you honestly think you could do that?"

"Chief," answer Ryder, "I do not think it. I know it." He shoved his composition book across the table toward me. "How do you like my cats? Do you think I show any bump for drawing?"

"No. Ryder, how would you feel about taking up with Mama and Lyman and me in a permanent way?"

Ryder pulled his composition book back and drew another cat. "Whose idea is that?"

"Mine."

"How old is it?"

"About ten minutes."

"If it is no older than that, then your brother and mama do not know about it."

"No, but I'm sure they would like it and be agreeable to it."

"You are after my know-how. Well, it's for sale. The question is, how much?"

"We would give you a piece of the property at Jewel Sink."

"You are a kid. I cannot dicker with a kid on anything this important."

"You don't have to. Lyman and Mama will make you the same offer as soon as I suggest it to them. I know they will."

"It would be a lot of hard work and I would have to do most of it. It is not a bad idea looking at it quick. But I don't know. I would have to give it my most carefulest consideration before jumping into it."

"If you give it your most carefulest consideration you would not be jumping into it."

"Now you are making fun of my English."

"Ryder, if you put in with Mama and Lyman and me in a permanent way, I would teach you how to read and write good English. We would study together in the evenings after our day's work was done. Could you teach me how to use a plowshare?"

"I might could."

"What is it?"

"What is what?"

"A plowshare."

"It's a farm tool. On ground like the kind out at Jewel Sink you would want to use a jumper plow. I noticed a lot of old snags and stumps out there, and so a jumper would be the best. Where would we study in the evenings after our day's work was done?"

"In your little house. In your little parlor. There would not be anything improper in that but, if my being there alone with you made you uneasy, you could come up to the main house instead. Mama would be there to chaperone us. I just thought the parlor of your own little place would give us more privacy."

"I don't remember but one house at Jewel Sink," said Ryder.

I said, "There is the big house and there are some out-buildings. We would fix up one of those for you. One of them has a fireplace and you could cook in that when you didn't want to eat with us. Of course you would always be most welcome to do that when you felt like it. And we could do something about the owls if they disturbed your rest too much."

"Owls do not bother me," answered Ryder. In his eyes something was growing. The lobby of the Packard Hotel was still as a museum.

Chapter Four

Mama grew thoughtful when Ryder and I went to her with our proposal. Lyman was scornful and balked. He slammed out but the next day was back with a hired car and drove all of us out to Jewel Sink. There was no alliance with him during the drive. He was sarcastic and humiliated and angry. He said what we owned at Jewel Sink belonged to the snakes. That it was a trash heap and only trash would even consider living in it. We would see. He would prove it to us. There were cases of erysipelas in Church Falls and we were wasting his valuable time.

The house at the Sink showed its many years of neglect. There was decay and sag. In some of the rooms the wind whistled through the chinks in the walls.

Lyman took one look at the cooking stove in the kitchen and said, "Oh, impossible! This whole notion is impossible."

"We are not here to speak of the impossible," flamed Mama. "We are here to look at the possible. I am not afraid of this place. Your father and I lived in worse than this when we were first married. It has potential. The taxes have been paid on it for this year so there is no threat there." She and Ryder inspected the stove and neither turned a hair. In a family manner Ryder said he could fix it. He removed its lids and peered at its innards, and got down on his knees and looked at its iron legs. He was a good salesman and, at last, even Lyman was grudgingly convinced.

When we got back to the Packard Hotel, Lyman drew up a homemade document, later to be properly executed by a lawyer, which gave Ryder deed to two acres of the land at Jewel Sink plus free use of one of the outbuildings for a period of a year, arranged for credit at three stores to be extended to us, handed Mama a hundred dollars in cash, and went back to caring for his patients.

That evening after supper I sat with Ryder in his corner of the Packard lobby. His head and his composition book were full of ideas. He and Mama and I had made up a list of the supplies and equipment we thought we would need to set up living at Jewel Sink, making every effort to keep it sensible. Ryder would not let it alone but kept erasing and adding and subtracting. He spelled mirror like this: Meer.

I said, "What's a meer?"

"It's what you look at yourself in."

"That isn't how you spell it."

"I don't care. I know what I mean."

"I thought you wanted to learn about words."

"I do, but I don't want a lesson now. Stop making me nervous."

"How am I making you nervous?"

"I don't know, but stop it."

"You're a curious man."

"How do you mean that?"

65

"You're odd. Have you ever been married?"

"No."

"You told me one time you ditched a female. Why did you do it?"

"She was no-account and I was no-account. We was both better off without each other."

"You told me you were eighty. How old are you really?"

"Chief," said Ryder, "I do not clutter up my mind with dabs like that."

"You don't know, do you? You told me you were ten when your father and mother told you to hit the door. If you knew what year that was, you could count backward and find out what age you are now."

"And that might make me feel bad," said Ryder. "It do not make one particle. To you my face might look like it has already wore out two bodies, but that is because you are a kid. Why are you grizzling me like this? Your mama and brother is satisfied with my credentials."

"I think you are somewhere around twenty-four or twenty-five."

"It is a free country. Uncle Whiskers has not got around yet to telling us what we can think." Ryder bent to his composition book, possessed by its smudged sheets. "I keep looking at this list. We don't want to forget anything when we do our buying tomorrow."

"Have you a weapon on your list there? There are wild cats and panthers in the hills around Jewel Sink. I have never seen any of either out there, but that is what they say."

"I own a rifle and a pair of pistols," said Ryder. He had cropped his hair and he wore a clean brown and white checked gingham shirt. He drew one of his fireside cats. "I am glad your brother agreed to let you and me do all the moving and him bring your mama on out afterward. I could not feature her riding out of town on muleback or behind one. She is a true lady. I wished we could leave the mule off our list, but we will need both him and the horse and, if we get them now, we will save money. Mules and horses is always cheaper in winter than spring. I am not like most people. I always think ahead."

I said, "Ryder, I would like to see your guns sometime."

"You ought to pick yourself something better to be curious about," said Ryder.

"I think I ought to learn how to handle a gun. What if some night an escaped homicidal maniac or somebody like that comes and breaks in on Mama and me? Mama would not know what to do."

"Your Mama is not the weak little sister you think she is," said Ryder.

"I had better sleep with a rolling pin beside my bed. I don't think I would be much good at hand-to-hand combat, though."

"Protecting you and your mama is part of the bargain," said Ryder. "I am going to string up a rope between your house and mine, and tie some cans and a cowbell to it. Then, if a prowler comes, all you will have to do is jerk it and I will come running. I sleep light."

"Have you ever killed anybody?"

"I do not recollect, Chief."

"What are we going to raise on our land at Jewel Sink?"

"Whatever will keep us eating and bring us the most money. I have been doing some thinking on that. Most of them apple trees out there is wore out and was not planted in the right spots in the first place. Some of the ground out there is bad gullied."

"Are you going to put me behind the plowshare?"

"No. I am going to let you stick to your dolls and my education. I might let you help me plant a few spuds in your spare time."

"How did it happen you killed somebody?"

"It happened."

"Where?"

"New Mexico."

"You are well traveled, aren't you?"

"I have been around some."

"Were you sorry about it afterward?"

"I lost a few winks over it till I found out my victim was wanted over in Arizona for the murder of the judge who sent his brother up to do a life sentence for the joy killings of two of our first Americans. They was women and, to make it worse, they both had their papoose cubs with them. They said the little ones set beside their dead mamas for two days before they was found. My victim thought I was one of the jury members who had helped to send his brother to the pen. He had vowed to get them all. When he came up on me, I saw right away he was not there to swap friendly words. It was in the mountains and was so still you could hear the lizards chasing their suppers. He came out of the brush with his pistol drawed and he was yelling like some crazy. We each fired at the same time. I was lucky. Well, that is all history now and bad history at that. I don't know how you roped me into telling you this. I never told anybody else."

"Not even the authorities? What did you do with the victim's body?"

"I am through talking, Chief. You have got sand in your eyes and had better get on up to your little bed. Good night. Don't let the bedbugs bite. If they do, take your shoe and knock them black and blue."

I thought that was funny but unnecessary advice. The Packard Hotel did not have bugs in its beds.

The next day was raw and wet, made of that stiff stuff that chews away at the Atlantic coastline all the way from Nova Scotia down to the tip end of Florida. Mama said she just knew the people over on the Georgia seaboard were taking a pounding. Ryder ignored the weather. He had a pleasant time haggling with the man who sold us our horse and mule. He was a shrewd bargainer. After two hours of cat-and-mouse play, our seller, sorely tested, agreed to throw in one used saddle and accessories and lend us a four-wheeled, closed-body wagon for a period of two days. Then we went to a hardware store, where we bought an assortment of carpenter's tools, some cheap cooking and eating utensils, a washboard and wash pot, a pair of sadirons, and a round, portable bathtub made of some kind of metal. Ryder said

he would need a shaving mirror which he would pay for out of his own pocket. The storekeeper set three mirrors on his counter, and Ryder took his time in making his selection. While he was doing that, Tom Clegg Senior came in. With an outstretched hand, the storekeeper rushed to greet him. "Mr. Clegg, sir. How are you?"

"I am all right," said Clegg.

"I will be with you in a minute," bellowed the merchant, bounding back to Ryder. "You know Mrs. Commander and her daughter, and this gentleman is Ryder Tuttle."

Clegg looked at Mama and with his right hand touched the brim of his hat. "Madam." To Ryder he said, "How do you do," but did not offer to shake his hand.

Ryder took his introduction to Clegg at face value. He thought Clegg really wanted to know how he did. So he said, "Well, I got no kicks today. Me and Mrs. Commander and Lucy here is on our way to taking up living at Jewel Sink."

"Indeed," said Clegg. He did not bat an eye.

"Yessir," chirped Ryder, and turned back to the counter.

Beautiful and remote and untouchable Mama stood holding the newly purchased washboard in her arms. She had only nodded to Clegg. Ryder asked her to hold the mirrors up one by one so that he could test his image in each. In a minute, he made his decision and the merchant snatched up his pencil and added the mirror to our list of charges. He was nervous and had to figure the total of the bill twice. After that was done, Ryder told him the mirror did not belong on it and he had to make an adjustment. He was more interested in entertaining Clegg than he was in selling us anything else. There was a fire burning in the stove in the center of the room, but it was not making much headway toward drying out the air.

Clegg brushed raindrops from his lapels and the storekeeper, while packing our purchases in cardboard boxes, attempted to make conversation with the moneylender. "I heard you sent your boy off to military school."

"Yes," said Clegg.

"He will make good on it," crowed the storekeeper. "No way for him not to, him being half Clegg and half Summerhill. One day this town will see young Tom come home a general in our country's army, and we will all have to close down business for the day and set our flags out and put on a big parade."

Clegg said, "Shep, I think I will let my business with you go until tomorrow. I have an important appointment with my attorney and am already late for it."

The merchant was crestfallen. He said, "As you wish, sir, of course." He sped out from behind the counter and toward the door. He opened it for the moneylender and stood, letting the rain, which was coming down slantwise, drench his front. Water was beating against the store's panes and the trees lining both sides of the street were being whipped by the wind. It was all natural. I watched Clegg go to the center of the street and pause there waiting for two vehicles to pass. The blowing water and the running clouds were marvelous, yet Clegg did not look up nor to his right or left. He was out of harmony with the scene.

The next morning, two hours after dawn, Ryder and I rode out of Church Falls—he handling the mule drawing the loaded wagon and I on horseback. Our storm had blown itself out. I told Ryder I had named the horse Mary, and he looked down on me from his plank wagon seat and said, "You ride her like you was born on her back."

"Papa sent me to riding school when I was ten," I said. "I used to go for lessons every Friday afternoon. Papa bought me a riding habit. He liked me to look pretty. He used to come and watch me take the jumps."

Said Ryder, "You liked your papa, didn't you?"

"I loved him. I still do."

"After a while it will get easier for you," said Ryder.

The town was behind us now. There were mud ponds in our road and the sun had topped the hills. I said, "No."

"It will," insisted Ryder.

I said, "It will not because I will not let it. I am not like most people."

"I have noticed that," observed Ryder. "Well, we all got a little throwback in us."

"I don't know what you mean."

"Somebody told me your Grandma Commander was a ring-tooter in her day."

"I never knew her."

"They say one time a drummer passing through Jewel Sink ran over one of her roosters by mistake and did not bother to stop. Your grandma got a good look at his face, though, and a couple of years later, when he made the mistake of passing by her house again, he got himself baptized in Jewel Springs. He was only a little thimble and she was one of them big scrappy types. They say she had it all over him when it came to size. The way I heard it, it was winter and he had to do all the work hisself. There wasn't no singing or praying. I bet the next time he ran over a rooster he thought twice."

I said, "I don't know if I believe that story. It sounds made up."

"Hell doesn't have no fury like a wronged woman," said Ryder, and clucked to his mule.

With my hand I gave Mary a slap on her flank and we galloped away, beating Ryder to Jewel Sink by at least an hour. He and I worked all afternoon unloading the wagon and making our house and the building that was to serve as Ryder's home as livable as we could. We brought the picnic table and benches in and, at Ryder's suggestion, I scrubbed these pieces down with some lye soap which Ryder produced from his trunk. It made my hands tingle and turn red. In our sleeping rooms we spread dried pine needles on the bare floors and laid our new cotton mattresses down. Ryder said he had never become accustomed to sleeping between sheets, that he preferred blankets under him and over him.

At duskfall Lyman came with Mama. He was itching for reasons to dissolve the plan to live at Jewel Sink, but

to each of his fretting objections Mama had one that coun-
tered. She said, "Your grandparents lived here and so shall
we."

"It isn't the same," argued Lyman. "Even in your poor-
est days with Papa I doubt if you lived like this."

"Then I shall learn," said Mama. "We all will."

And so, holding to that sort of strange human material
by which people find new powers and create new securities
in this miracle we call living, we did.

Jewel Sink received us warily. We had to find out how
to take possession of it and heed its details and warnings.
One night Mama and I heard what we thought was a woman
shrieking in the faraway stillness. I jumped from my bed
and jerked on the signaling rope Ryder had strung between
our house and his. The cowbell and clusters of cans attached
to it made an awful racket and Ryder, clad only in baggy
long johns which was his nightwear, came on the run. He
said the shrieker was a "mountain-screamer" and the animal was only having himself a singing lesson.

Mama curtained our windows with cheap, flimsy material, and frequently small animals crept up onto the outside sills and peered in. During those first nights in our
new home, Mama and I kept a candle burning in a bowl of
water in our bedroom. One morning, while drawing water
from the well to carry to the house, I saw what I thought was
a dog. As I turned from the well and started up the path
toward the house, it leaped out from behind a clump of
naked bushes to my right and streaked away. It was red.
Ryder said it was a fox.

Ryder was good company most of the time, an entertaining talker and a good listener, but during our conversations he would not let me dwell on the subject of Papa's absence. He did not know, because none of us had told him, the full truth behind our move from Church Falls to Jewel Sink. He knew that we had lost what we had owned through financial reverses. He did not know about Mr. Clegg.

The other secret, my secret, shared only with Marion and Delia, I carried about with me, guarding it as one guards a religious belief questionable to others. It was my religion. I knew what I wanted from it and, faithful to it, I fed it promises: *When the time comes. When it does.*

Once or twice a week Lyman came bringing us fresh milk and a supply of whatever fresh fruits and vegetables were available. When he could spare the time he would eat with us, and then he and Ryder would walk out and look at the land. In the spring, said Ryder, he would break ground and make it ready for planting. The gullies and old roots would go, the seeds would be dropped, and then we would begin to see something.

Soon Lyman did not doubt Ryder's abilities, for Jewel Sink had changed the ex-trunk peddler. When he talked of his plans, all of us could almost see the greening fields and smell the newly turned earth which the sun and air would sweeten.

Lyman began to lose some of his stern and standoffish ways. One of his "hello girl" patients, who was either called or ordered out of town on short notice, left a forgotten coat in his office and her unpaid bill on his desk. Lyman brought the coat to me. It was hunter red with an attached hood. It was a mile too big for me, and I told Lyman I would not wear it. "I already have enough coats and, besides, I do not like where this one has been."

"Where it has been has nothing to do with you," said Lyman. "You need a wrap to rough around in. You had better learn to save your good things. The Lord only knows when I will be able to buy you more."

So I wore the coat to the woods to gather firewood for the kitchen stove and the fireplaces. I helped Ryder knock down one of the smaller outbuildings, and we used some of the lumber it yielded to build a wash shed. Ryder set up a clothesline at the rear of the main house and showed Mama and me how to "stew" our clothing and bed linens and towels in a steaming black iron pot, and then fish them from the water with a pole, and carry them dripping to the shed, there to be either rinsed or given additional attention on the scrub board. Ryder seldom asked for my help or Mama's, but we gave it. There were repairs to the crumbled hearthways and the old clay-and-stick chimneys. Mama wished for a pantry and got one.

Our new way of life was a hardship to Mama but it did not coarsen her, it only strengthened. And I think it was this that Tom Clegg saw as he traveled through Jewel Sink, sometimes stopping his car in the road that ran past our house. He and his driver would both alight, and the driver would raise the hood of the car pretending to be looking for some trouble while Clegg walked up and down. Clegg knew the art of this cheap ceremony, had the bold knack for hitching it all together. He saw our newly whitewashed house standing rescued and courageous. He saw Mama at the clothesline, still a belle, with her skirt drawn back from her body by the wind. She stooped and straightened and pinned and she was a part of the wind. She was life and that kind of pledge not often seen in fair and delicate women. She had will and took no notice of Clegg or his man or the car in the road.

Ryder did. He went out and offered Clegg his assistance and came back rebuffed. He said, "I don't mix up very easy, but that man made me feel like the little boy what dropped his chewing gum in the chicken house. Who is he?"

"He's nobody, but his name is Tom Clegg. You were introduced to him that day we were all in the hardware store buying supplies. How did he strike you?"

Ryder thought. "Like a man eating a grindstone. Have we got something that belongs to him?"

"Of course not."

"He acts like we have."

"He's a good actor."

"I don't like the way he looks at your mama."

"Then next time why don't you punch him in the face?"

"I don't like the way he looks at you either. Have you and him had trouble?"

"No."

"That day we was in the hardware store there was some talk about a son. I remember now. Do you know him?"

"We are acquainted. He used to come to our house and sit in a corner when his father and mine had business to conduct. His hair grows in instead of out, and he doesn't dare sneeze without asking his father's permission first. Mr. Clegg is a moneylender. The day Papa was killed, he was with him. We haven't had much to do with him since."

"Well," observed Ryder, "I can't blame you for that. He looks like a man who doesn't like himself. People who don't even like themselves make terrible company. Usually they're mean." He stood the bookcase he was making for Mama upright. It had a curved top. Ryder was clever with wood and at managing solutions to the endless problems that confronted. He was not good at gaining the education he said he wanted. In the evenings, while Mama read her own books, I tackled that thankless and maddening job. Ryder was not an apt or cooperative pupil. I said, "You don't clumb a tree. You climb a tree. You climb it. If you say you clumbed it again I am going to give up on this and you may stay ignorant for all I care."

"I heard a little knowledge is a dangerous thing," said Ryder. "And I think that is right, but I ain't satisfied with myself either way."

"Our language is beautiful when spoken correctly," I said. "It's like poetry."

"I know a poem," said Ryder, and chanted, "Peter Rogers eats fish, alligators catch eels, eels catch alligators, fish eat raw potatoes."

He and I made an agreement whereas every time I caught him saying "ain't" he would pay me a penny. At the end of the first day he owed me fifty cents. When I ordered him to pay, he said he didn't have the coin on him and threw his wadded vocabulary lesson into the fire. We were all sick of the winter's complaining and were longing to see the first signals of spring.

Our roof was tight. Wood from the woods all around us fed our fires daylong. We ate. And worked. And slept. And each of us mused upon our own visions, holding them close.

Chapter Five

Came Marion and Delia one moonless night. Mama was busy with her sewing in our house and Ryder and I were in his cabin wrangling and hassling over one of his lessons when the rap on his door sounded. Ryder bounded up and went to open it, and there they stood, anxious and apologetic and humbled as I had never seen them. They had walked the whole distance from Church Falls carrying almost everything they owned in two wicker baskets and two long, cloth sacks. Marion looked ready to topple. As he set his basket and sack on the floor just inside Ryder's door, I saw the trembling in his shoulders and hands. He said, "We spied your mama by her lamp in your big house, but then we saw your light and figured to come on back here first with our trouble."

I said, "What is wrong?"

Delia had a smile ready. She removed her wool shawl and stood with it draped over one arm. "We've been let out of our place in Church Falls and can't find another. It's a riddle to us. It's as though all of a sudden our reputations are at question. Whew. That was some walk. I told Marion we should have started out earlier, but he wouldn't hear me. We thought Lyman could bring us out here in Doctor Porter's buggy and waited and waited for him, but he didn't come back. Doctor Porter said he didn't know where he had gone." Ryder had put himself into motion, had taken Delia's shawl and Marion's coat and drawn both wayfarers to his fireside bench. Then he rushed to his kitchen and came back bearing a bottle of vanilla and a tin cup. Delia drank a little of the liquid and made a face. Marion's portion made his eyes water.

I said, "In a minute I'll go and tell Mama you are here. She will say that you are to stay with us. You said Doctor Porter told you he didn't know where Lyman was?"

"Doctor Porter didn't know where he was himself," said Marion. "He was piled up in his bed and it looked to me like he had been there a while. We had to near about knock his door down to wake him up."

Delia had her hands outstretched to the blaze in front of her. "Lucy, we think something has gone wrong for Lyman."

"What makes you think that?"

"We think it because we must have made twenty trips to his office looking for him. Off and on we looked all day yesterday and much of today. He is gone and so is Doctor Porter's horse and buggy. Doctor Porter told us he thought Lyman went off up into the hills with some men. He thinks that was two days ago."

"Two days ago? Lyman went off up into the hills two days ago with some men and hasn't come back?" I stood up and took a step toward Ryder.

"Halloo," said Ryder. "Now wait a minute. Let's not

get all creeped up when chances are there is not anything to get creeped up over. Doctors is not like ordinary people. They go when and where they are called. When it comes to time, they lose track of it quicker than a white dog when they are off treating somebody sick. One time, when I was out in Wyoming, I hired out to one. He didn't know his way around the mountains and paid me to go with him. We was four days seeing to our victims once we found them, but if it hadn't been for the doctor's wife I would have only been paid for two."

I said, "Oh, you always have a story for everything. Doctors live by their watches. Can you not understand simple English? My brother has been gone for two days, and Marion and Delia here think there's something wrong."

"That do not make it true," said Ryder, angling for some think time.

"There is such a thing as human intuition. Do you know what that is?"

"I've heard of it."

"I don't think you have. Intuition is when you know something without seeing it. It warns you. It tells you things. Maybe you came without any, but I did not. Mine tells me now that there is some trouble with my brother, and what are we going to do about it? Just stand here all night and talk about white dogs?"

"White dogs," said Ryder, and looked at the bottle of vanilla in his hand. "Chief, we are not talking about white dogs. We are talking about Lyman. I only mentioned that white dog to show you how you get fussed up over things too fast. A white dog don't do that. He ponders over things first and that is what you should do."

"There is nothing to ponder," I said. "I am going to Church Falls and I am going now. Do I go alone or will you go with me?"

"I am not going to Church Falls tonight," said Ryder, "and neither are you. It is blacker than a stack of black cats out there, and there is big holes in the road from all the rain, and a mule or a horse don't see any better than you or me in the dark. There is no cure for one with a broke leg but to shoot him. Would you like to see that?"

"No."

"Then," said Ryder, "here is what we'll do. First we'll go and tell your mama that these friends of ours are here. Tonight they can have my bed and I will sleep out here on the floor. Tomorrow I will think of a different plan."

"We have our own bedding," offered Delia, "but had to leave it in Lyman's office. I pinned a note to it so he'd know what it was."

"If you did that," reasoned Ryder, "then your thoughts about there being something gone wrong with Lyman is not as strong as you said a minute ago. Everything smells like trouble when you are tired and don't know where you are going to lay your head next. Now I will have the rest of my say. We will not mention anything to Mrs. Commander about Lyman tonight. We will just tell her that Marion and Delia have come to stay with us until they can stand up by themselves again. If I know her, she will be glad. It will not hurt any of us to pull our belts in a little more."

"Marion and I have a little money," said Delia, and Ryder planted a mellow look on her and took a little swig from his vanilla bottle. It was a deep and beautiful thing to watch Mama's reunion with Marion and Delia. We had a heavy frost that night.

The next morning Ryder and I rode into Church Falls, he aboard his mule and Mary and I cantering alongside. We had told Mama we were going after some nails and the bedding Marion and Delia had left in Lyman's office. Our stomachs were full of Delia's cornmeal pancakes, and Ryder sang silly songs. We watched the fat sun change from orange to yellow, and Ryder said, "Well, I see God has got his britches on again." I thought that was irreverent and made a mental note to include some biblical teachings in future educational sessions.

We went into Church Falls unsung and clattered our way through its genteel streets, not all of them yet fully ready for their day. I caught glimpses of our reflections in the storefront windows, Ryder on his blanketed mule and me astride my little mare, the hem of my red coat flapping around my calves. And I thought, Well, Lucy Commander, you have come a way sure enough. Where did that stranger go, that one who used to be you, so vain and prissy?

Doctor Porter's place had undergone a slight face cleaning, the kind a masculine hand would give, yet still it had not quit being a comment on what sort of man its owner was. Ryder and I left our mounts hitched to a tree in a little scrap of meadow across from it.

The offices of Doctors Porter and Commander were unoccupied of people. Ryder and I lingered in them only for a minute. I saw the pile of bedding Marion and Delia had left. Its note to Lyman was still attached to the roll with a safety pin. Ryder and I then went through all the other rooms in the building. There was nobody there. We came back to the offices.

I said, "I think there is something peculiar here."

Spoke Ryder, "Chief, I have just found out something about you. Your mind is always hell-after-the-pullet. I do not see a thing peculiar. It's all reasonable except you." He was in a pique and went over to the pile of bedding and began separating it, making two bundles of it, while I prowled around.

Ryder completed his task and carried both piles of bedding across the street to our horse and mule, while I sat at the desk I assumed to be Lyman's and penned a note asking him to come to Jewel Sink as soon as he returned from wherever he was.

I left the note propped against an inkwell, and then Ryder and I went after the nails we didn't really need. Our seller was one of Papa's old acquaintances, and I asked him if he happened to know where Doctor Porter and Lyman were hiding out. With his eye on his scale he replied, "They aren't hiding out. Why would they do that? I saw Lyman yesterday. I think it was yesterday. Maybe it was the day before though. The days have got to where they run by me like hours anymore. I saw Doctor Porter in the Blue Chip Cafe a couple of hours ago. He was with the sheriff. One of them bought me my second cup of coffee. They both had been up all night. There was a knifing over at Glenda's dance hall last evening, and now I guess the piano player and one of Glenda's girls are sitting it out in the jailhouse. They were planning on marrying. The hitch was that she already is. To somebody else. You want me to put these nails on your bill?"

Ryder said, "Yes," and took the sack and we left the store. Ryder was still in a perverse mood. I asked him to go back to Lyman's office with me and wait around, and he refused. He also refused to go with me to see the sheriff. He said, "What for? The sheriff is not your brother's nursemaid. You think he's going to drop what he is doing and go running off to the hills on a goose chase, when chances are the goose is right this minute sitting by somebody's bed looking at a case of measles? Even if you could talk the sheriff into it, where would you expect him to start looking? There is about seventy miles of hills out there. I know because I've walked most of them."

I stood for a minute beside Mary, hugging my arms and doubting. I watched Ryder swing himself up onto his mule, and I saw the old secure street before me. Mary nuzzled my shoulder and the doubt in me drained. We went home. I told Mama that we had missed Lyman, but that he would come home when he could, that I had left him a note asking him to do so. Delia and Marion were up to some of their old good stuff. Delia was giving everything in sight a cleaning, and Marion had located a cache of old farm implements in our barn and was removing the rust from the pieces. There was good talk that night at our dinner table. I kept listening for Lyman and though he did not come still the doubt in me stayed quiet.

It was back the next morning, the question of it turning and turning in my mind. I thought I would get Ryder to one side and speak to him about it, make another appeal to him. But Delia, serving me my breakfast, said that he and Marion had taken the mule and gone to the apple orchard lying a quarter mile to the west of the house. "They took their lunch with them," she said. "While he's got Marion here to help him, Ryder wants to take out some of those old trees so he can plan where to put new ones. Your mama woke up with a cold and a sore throat and I made her go back to bed." Skillet in hand, she went back to the stove and I saw the bend in her shoulders. During her brief time away from us some of the old snap and crackle had gone out of her. Now she was servile and in the corners of her eyes there was apprehension disciplined but there. And I thought, I can't do it. I can't ask her to go with me. I'll have to go alone.

Delia was making cocoa for Mama and, when she left the kitchen to take it to her, I put some dried prunes, a handful of raisins, and a buttered biscuit in a sack and went out the back door. Mary came trotting to meet me and I led her around to the barn where she ate and then to the water trough where she drank. While she was about that I went to Ryder's cabin and, after a minute's searching, found his pistols. I did not know how to open its shell chamber, so I could not tell whether the one I selected was loaded or not. It had a gilt handle and its weight between my belt and my ribs was a discomfort. As soon as I was astride Mary, I transferred the weapon to one of the saddlebags.

We went through the winter-bare orchard lying north of the house, and then there were the acres and acres of the wildness before us. For a change the air was blue. I judged the temperature to be about fifty degrees. Mary was in a mood to run and I let her. We raced through natural wood valleys and across the brown and rutted marches to where the curve of the hills met the prairie.

We went up and up and then Mary, winded, had to stop and investigate holes and twigs and rocks. She came upon a skeleton of a bird and I dismounted to give my legs some exercise. The hills were silent. In their sweeps and timbered sprawls they concealed, but they did not say what.

This was aborigine land. There were no signs of civilization among its bluffs and ridges, no trails, no riffles of smoke rising from its glades. I remembered Ryder saying that he had walked most of it and I wondered why since, all around, as far as the eye could see, there was only the undisturbed and natural picture, the landscape untouched by fire or axe. It was that kind of scenery that calms and dwarfs, and now I could not think that Lyman was somewhere out there sitting in a cabin beside a sickbed. Yet I led Mary on up a way before deciding I was on a fool's errand.

There came a shift in the weather with cold air currents streaming down through the tunnels of the upper peaks. The air began to darken momently and, mounted again, I said to Mary, "Well, fiddle. It is going to rain or do something. We had better start back." We turned around and found our trace and began to descend.

Halfway down our incline, I reined Mary in and we stopped, for there at its foot were two men on horseback parading back and forth. There was too much space between us for me to make any judgment concerning them. There was no reason to even attempt judgment. The prairie stretching out before me, wild and free in all directions, was no man's land, a faunal province without a boss. The men were merely having a little game, engaging in some kind of play-ritual. So spoke my thoughts.

Separately and accurately the riders wheeled and passed each other again and again until, at last, they came together at the foot of my hill and sat there in an attitude of confidence and waiting, looking up at me like mischievous boys. They were blocking my passage. There were wicked-looking boulders on both sides of me and, except to turn and ascend again, I could not change my direction.

Through my head there went the faint notion that the two horsemen might be mistaking me for someone else, possibly the original owner of the red coat I wore. At all events it was either advance or retreat, so I nudged Mary and we went down and when I was within conversation distance I said "You are blocking my way. Kindly move and let me pass."

They were opposites, one big and one little. People who make up stories about their kind always give them identifying marks. Cheek scars, missing earlobes, pig eyes, blackened teeth, beards. Things like that. These two had none of those. The smaller one had a full, smooth face studded with eyes that surely had never looked upon anything shocking or brutal. The big one might have been the poetical village smithy. The least one went by the name of Penn and the smithy by the name of Orlie. Each wore a hip gun and both horses carried a sheathed rifle attached to their saddles and what I thought might be other trappist gear. The horses were indifferent. They swung their big heads back and forth.

"Penn," said the smithy, "the little lady wants to pass."

"To where, Orlie?" asked Penn. "There's not anything out there to pass to but dirt and rocks and old dried up grass."

"She wants to pass," said Orlie, all indolence and fond of his role, and I realized then that I was the object of their game and, whatever it was, whatever it was for, it was not a piece of mere mischief. These two were out after some gain. They watched me and they were relaxed, but I saw their clear and disciplined thinking.

I said, "My name is Lucy Commander. I live at Jewel Sink. You will please step aside and let me pass."

"Oh," said Penn, "we cannot do that."

I said, "You had better and you had better be quick about it, too. My big brother knows I am out here and he will be riding out to meet me shortly. Be warned that if you try any funny business with me he will not be easy with you."

"Orlie," said Penn, "did you have in mind to try any funny business with this here girl?"

Answered Orlie, "You could not hire me to harm one hair on her darling little head."

I asked, "What do you want with me? You will move and let me pass at once if you know which side of your face your nose is pasted on and want it to stay there."

"Turn your horse around," ordered Penn.

"I will not. Why should I?"

"Unless you would rather walk to where you're going."

"I am not going anywhere with you two nothings. If you force me to do so, you will be sorry to your dying day. I am from a respectable family, and who do you think will be believed when you are dragged in for kidnapping? The judge will sentence you both to rock piles for the rest of your natural lives."

Orlie lost his temper. "We are not going to be dragged anywhere. We are not kidnapping you. We found you out here wandering around suffering from a temporary loss of memory. You could not tell us who you were so us, being the good samaritans we are, rescued you and took you with us back to our camp. You feel that lump on your head?"

"There's no lump on my head."

"You got it when you fell from your horse, and that is what caused you to forget who you were or where you come from," said Penn.

"Is it your intention to give me the lump that is not there now?"

"How you behave will decide that," said Orlie. The blue air was gone. It had started to drizzle. All three horses

91

were fidgeting. I said, "All right. You have convinced me that it is to my advantage to act sensibly. I will go with you peacefully, but first please give me a minute to adjust my right stirrup. Perhaps one of you would be kind enough to do it for me?" The stirrup story was a ruse. What I really designed to do was to reach down and grab Ryder's pistol from my saddlebag and, if necessary, shoot my way out of the mess, but Orlie was not taking his eyes off me.

"With females it is always something," observed Penn, and he slid from this horse and came toward me. When he was in what I judged to be just the right distance, I let him have it square in his face with my booted right foot, and at the same time with my left one gave Mary the kick of her life. She jumped forward only missing Penn by a couple of inches. He fell to the ground howling and holding both hands to his nose. He was cursing me. My boot had not missed its mark. Mary and I shot down the hill but did not make it past Orlie. He wheeled his horse sideways and when we hit I was thrown, landing face downward in a cluster of sharp stones. I got my head lump then, but it was a few seconds before I fully realized it.

I saw Mary standing stunned and I saw Orlie reach for her reins. He said, "Come here!" But the little mare recovered her breath and, with the counterinstinct of survival, backed off, whirled, and without even a backward glance for me went streaking away. The drizzle was turning into a serious downpour.

Penn was on his feet and hollering to Orlie. "Let the horse go! She will work to our benefit!" His nose was purple and bloodied and tears of pain stood in his eyes. He came toward me and stood over me. "Get up."

I said, "I am hurt. I think one of my ribs is broken and I cannot see."

Penn yanked me to my feet and hustled me over to one of the horses. On the way he slapped me twice. I had lost my hat. My vision was blurred and there was a pain in my side which was making me feel faint. There was a quick re-arrangement of gear, and then I was hefted none too gently to the back of Orlie's animal and away we went, up and up, I holding on to the rider in front of me.

When we reached the hill's summit a halt was called, the men dismounted and held a conference to which I was not privy, then they boarded their horses again. We traveled a distance, first to the right and then to the left, and then went down a steep grade into an intermountain valley. My abductors did not talk and I could not. There was blood in my mouth and hair and with every jolt the pain in my side jabbed. The wind at our backs was cold and the rain in our faces was colder. In a palisade of evergreen grove and wintered brush we stopped for a few minutes. The men talked, trying to decide whether to go on or sit the weather out where we were.

Rough as it had been, the long ride had somewhat cleared my head. I watched Penn and Orlie jump to the ground. They started away from me and I called out to them, "Are you going to leave me here on this steed? I am sick to my stomach and cannot see too well. If I fall you might have a murder on your hands."

Orlie came back and lifted me from the horse. "You got that lump I said you'd get if you didn't behave yourself. Be careful you don't birth it a twin. Penn has got a strong temper and don't think anything about hitting females. He has got his pride same as you."

I said, "Neither of you knows the first thing about pride. If you did, you wouldn't be mixed up in whatever this is."

Orlie grinned. "There is all kinds of pride. Just you watch yours and see it don't get out of hand again. If it does, you might see it in the dust."

As words spoken at one time supply the recollection of another, providing a missing link, Orlie's threat caught at me. *Pride in the dust.* I had heard Tom Clegg using those very words on Mama, and now here was this man named Orlie mouthing it.

Orlie was watching me. "Did you hear what I said?"

And, on guard, I answered, "I heard."

"You don't look so good."

"That makes two of us."

"There is a creek down through them trees yonder. Maybe you had better get yourself down there and put some water on that lump and drink some, too. Give me your word you won't try anything and I will give you a few minutes to yourself."

I said, "You have it. I don't want a bullet in my back. Where are we going?"

Replied Orlie, "Oh, don't worry none about that. You leave the plans to Penn and me."

I thought I would be crafty. "Is that his right name?"

"No," answered Orlie. "His right name is Tom Thumb but don't let on I told you so." The expression in his eyes was soft and level.

I went down through the clustered pines and found the creek which was not a creek but a rapid flowing river issuing from some point up ahead. Against its marge, its color was yellow. It looked deep. I wobbled down to its edge and knelt and bathed my face and rinsed blood from my mouth. The water was not bad tasting. The rain had soaked my coat and washed my hair. It was slackening. Orlie only allowed me about ten minutes before hollering for me to come. He and Penn had decided we would go on. It was nearly dusk before we reached our destination.

Chapter Six

It rose up out of the wet dimness to meet us, ugly of effect, a lone and time-bitten building seated on a point of land jutting into the river, curved like an oxbow, which we had followed throughout the latter part of our trek. In this location the stream was wide and less active.

The building belonged to the dusk and the man who came from it had a face like the dusk. He came toward the horses and stood in front of Orlie's and looked at me once. There was nothing in his eyes but sourness and the self-preservative smoulderings of a life gone bad. He wore a slicker and a slouch hat and carried a rucksack and an unlighted lantern. "What took you so long? You promised me I could get away from here 'fore dark and it's nigh that now."

"We got hung up in a little rescue work," explained Orlie. "Found this little lady here laying senseless in the hills. Her horse had throwed her and now she can't remember who she is or where she belongs. How is our guest doing?"

"I hadn't looked in on him since noon," said Slouch Hat. "Did you remember to bring me my tobacco?"

"I remembered it," replied Orlie, "but, like I say, we

ran into some trouble with this girl here and so didn't make it to town. I don't know what we'll use for our supper."

"That is your lookout," said Slouch Hat. "You can pay me now and I'll be shoving off while there's still some daylight left."

By this time, both Orlie and Penn were on the ground. Penn was unloading his horse. When his arms were full he started toward the building. There was a dock at its front and a moored rowboat.

I decided to at least let Slouch Hat know I had a tongue and could use it. I said, "Listen, river rat, if you don't know what you are doing, I will tell you. My name is Lucy Commander and my brother is Doctor Lyman Commander of Church Falls. These men are kidnappers. I am not here of my own free will. Help me and I will see to it that you are rewarded. Refuse to help me and I will see to it that you are punished right along with these other two. I have one of the finest memories in Georgia. I never forget anything done for me or against me. Now how would you like to think that over before you go any further with this?"

Slouch Hat's attention was unaroused. He did not even blink. There was no show of hostility or anything else between him and Orlie. Whatever their feelings for one another might have been was masked. Slouch Hat stuck his hand out and said to Orlie, "You've had your end of our bargain. Now I'll have mine."

"Sure," said Orlie, and he brought a little sheaf of currency from his pocket and began counting. When he got to twenty dollars he stopped and handed the bills over, and without a word Slouch Hat turned and began to make his way toward the dock. When he reached it, he stepped down to the boat anchored there, released its mooring line with the tip of one of its oars, and shoved off. The rain had run away from us.

There was something hypnotic about this whole proceeding. There was the gloom of the hour deepening by the minute, and now came a mist stealing across the river. Through the gloom and the mist I saw the boat moving out over the water, the man seated in it dipping his oars and pulling and then dipping and pulling again.

I saw Penn come from the shack and run down to the end of the dock. All in a second there was a little flash of flame at his shoulder and a sharp crack rang out. Soundlessly, the man in the boat fell sideways. The vessel tipped and the man slipped into the water. It closed over his head and then the water took command of the boat. In a minute it, too, was gone.

The horse under me stirred and Orlie, turning to look up at me, said, "Take your heels out of his belly. He don't like to be dug that way. Get down and help me unload the rest of this stuff."

Flat and dull, there came my voice. "You are a maniac."

"I never argue politics or religion or what people think about me," said Orlie. "Watch you don't slip in the mud. It would be a shame to mess up that pretty coat. No, you walk ahead of me and don't try any tricks."

Loaded to our chins with gear, we started toward the shack. I had decided that this place was an abandoned fish camp. Penn was still on the dock and Orlie called out to him to go take care of the horses. We walked between the dripping trees, and every step was to me a small agony.

Orlie noticed my irregular gait and said, "It's your own fault if you got a broke rib. Next time maybe you will think before you try to come up against me. This is not a play party."

I asked, "What is it?"

For answer, Orlie said, "I'm so hungry I could eat a raw Yankee," and cut around in front of me and mounted the steps to the shack. By this time it was full dark, but Orlie knew his way around. While I waited in the doorway, he located two kerosene lanterns and, as soon as he had their wicks lighted, he handed one to me and at the same time pointed to an inside door. "Go say hello to our other star boarder. You and him will have to share accommodations tonight. We'll have some supper soon as Penn and me can get organized."

Holding the lantern aloft, I entered the room. I heard the click of the door lock behind me snap into place. There was a figure lying on an army cot and, colorless and bent, it rose and Lyman's voice, horrified, came from it. "Oh, no!" He came to me and took the lantern from me, and I saw that his right hand was badly swollen and that he had a black eye.

It was not real and yet it was reality, chill and foul and so stabbingly felt. We sat on the cot and talked in whispers. I said, "Lyman, what is it? Why is it? Why are we here? Who are these men?"

He leaned toward me holding his right hand in his left. The flame in the lantern cast its yellow glow, and I saw him not as a protector or one to be consulted but as one whose defenses had been insulted and consumed. He looked weak and ashamed of being so. He was hurt, and the aristocratic fineness in him could not understand our situation, for he had a moral and compassionate mind. He could not meet this. He said, "I don't know. I don't know what this is all about or who those men are. I heard a shot. Did they kill the old man?"

"Yes. What happened to your eye and hand?"

"I fought with the one named Penn."

"Is your hand broken?"

"No, it's only badly sprained."

"How long have you been here?"

"How long? It seems forever. My watch is gone. I've lost track of the time. This is the third day I think."

"How did you get here?"

Lyman lay back on the cot. "I came in Doctor Porter's horse and buggy. It's out there somewhere."

"You came alone?"

"No. Those two men escorted me. They came to my office and said there was a man out here who was so sick he shouldn't be moved. They offered me a hundred dollars to come. I never saw them before. There was no sick man. I don't know what this is all about. Where is Mama?"

"Home. Marion and Delia are with her. They came yesterday. They've been let out of their places in Church Falls. Lyman, what is this? We've been kidnapped, but what's the reason? We have no money. Everybody who knows us knows that. And these men know you. They know you are a doctor. But what do we have that they want? Have they told you?"

"No."

"Lyman?"

"I'm so tired," said Lyman. "So tired." He closed his eyes and then we didn't talk anymore. The air in the room was old. There was a window, but it had been sealed over with crisscrossed boards. I thought we should pray but did not suggest to Lyman that we do so, he looked so bad, and I could think of no prayer words, could not separate the spiritual from the human. I thought of the man Penn had just murdered and wondered what had caused his twisted being. Did someone somewhere wait for him? A son or a daughter or wife? And when he did not come would there be worry? Fear? Tears? Oh, no matter about him. He had been just as ruthless as his conspirators, just as sinful.

The flame in the lantern sent up its dirty smoke and made eerie shadows on the walls and I, thinking back and back, once more heard in my mind the thin, subtle voice of growing conviction, this time more audible.

Beyond the locked door our captors moved about. They talked. Said Penn, "The old coot didn't leave us a whistle."

Said Orlie, "That's gratitude for you."

"Wait a minute," said Penn. "There's a box up there. You're taller than me. Lift it down and let's see what's in it."

Orlie was not so glum as his partner. In a minute he

101

laughed and said, "Pay dirt. Beans. Six cans. There's a little meal, too, and here's some salt."

Penn groaned. "We are both beginning to look like beans, but all right. Get the little squaw out here and let her work for her supper. Bring the croaker, too. I learnt him a lesson. He won't try anything again. Maybe he can do something about my nose. It's killing me."

Lyman sat up. He whispered an order. "Don't antagonize them. Do as they say."

I had not removed my coat, which was wet almost through to its lining. The door to the main room of the shack opened and Orlie poked his head in. "Come out and be sociable. You done sulked in here long enough. Little lady, I hope you can cook as good as you can kick."

There were a few old pieces of furniture in the hut's main room. In the contraption that passed for a stove there was a blaze going. Smoke curled from its flue and lid. The cornmeal in Slouch Hat's forgotten box was alive with bugs and, when I pointed them out to Orlie, he displayed some disgust and pitched the mess out the door.

With his good hand, Lyman examined Penn's nose and said, "It's only bruised. In a day to two the swelling will go down and it will return to its normal size and color."

Said Penn, "It had better." And ordered Lyman back to his prison.

I told Orlie I would like to go for a privacy before our bean supper, and he handed me a lantern. "Help yourself but don't be all night about it and, in case you get any notions about running off, remember we got your brother in there." From his pile of gear he had dug out a bottle of whiskey, and he and Penn were having turns nipping at it.

I went out into the night. The moon was up and the river water glistened in its reflection. I did not tarry for a second look at its strange peace. My desperate plan was to find something in the way of a weapon, a sharp stick or stone small enough to store in one of my pockets but big enough to use to advantage if the opportunity came.

Weather and wild and earth revolution had had their say to the land lying around the fish shack. At its back, mighty trees stood tip to tip and where they stopped, in the clefts watered by runnels trickling down from the uplands, there were folds of rock.

In one of the clearings I found a sharp, flat stone the size of a man's hand. As I stooped to lift it from its bed, I heard a sound that did not belong and looked up to see a shape moving toward me. It carried itself on two legs and as it drew nearer, in the stillness, in the moonlight, I saw that it was Ryder! With a finger to his lips he beckoned, and I grabbed up my lantern and we went back into the trees and stood behind the trunk of one.

Ryder was equipped. Under his open coat he wore a broad leather belt, which supported his two holstered pistols, and a sling on his shoulder was attached to his rifle.

I said, "What took you so long? And how did you know to come here?"

"Chief," said Ryder, "do not punch me like that again. I have been busier than a cat on a tin roof finding out things today that I should have knowed all along. Marion and me

103

got to be buddies this morning, and he told me all about the business with Mr. Tom Clegg and your daddy. And then Mary came ambling home alone and I rode out looking for you. I didn't think to find this, though. Who are those men in the shack?"

"I think they are in Tom Clegg's employ. I will tell you why I think so later. They have Lyman and they had an accomplice but, about an hour ago, I watched them kill him. Talk fast."

"Bless Pat!" exclaimed Ryder. "I knew that old boy. When I was a trunk peddler, he used to buy his tobacco off me whenever I would pass this way. I didn't know to come here. I just thought it would be a good place to spend the night in case I didn't find you, and this is where I wound up at. I got my mule and Mary both back there a ways, and Doctor Porter's horse and buggy are there, too. As you can see, I found the pistol you swiped from me. What kind of condition is Lyman in?"

"His right hand is out of commission and he has a black eye. Talk faster."

"I don't know as I can swallow that them buckaroos are in Tom Clegg's employ."

"Then don't. Swallow air. Swallow your Adam's apple. Swallow anything but, for heaven's sake, do something!"

"Are both them buckaroos in good shape?"

"They are and they are armed. Don't you understand? They are kidnappers! They brought Lyman here by force and then they did the same to me."

"Where is Lyman at the moment?"

"They have him imprisoned in a back room."

"Is it in line with the front door?"

"No. It's off to one side a little."

"Then," said Ryder, "here is what I am going to do. I am going to leave you here, and I am going to go up there and take them."

"Alone? Are you crazy? You can't take those two alone! That is not a plan, it's suicide! Give me one of your pistols. We will take them together. You see this rock? We will throw it at the door and, when they open it, we will have them cold."

"Now you are the one who is talking crazy. Take the lantern and git. Run back that way and you'll see Mary. Get on her and scat! Don't stop for nothin'! Go!"

"No. I'll not let you tackle this alone. Give me one of your pistols. Check it first to make sure it is fully loaded."

"Chief, I have not got any time to argue with you now."

"Then don't. Hand over one of the pistols. I don't expect those two ruffians to surrender without a good argument. They are not afraid of the devil so, when they open the door, we had better be ready. Give me one of the pistols."

"Chief, you don't know one end of a pistol from the other. You don't know anything. You are just a girl."

"I will know less than I do now, and so will you, if you don't do as I say. I don't want to kill anybody, but I don't want Lyman or any of the rest of us to die either. The pistol. Quickly!"

There was a moment when I thought he wouldn't do it.

Then he handed me the pistol, butt end first. He said, "Lucy."

"Come on! Let's go! Will this thing kick when I fire it? Confound you, Ryder, I told you I should learn how to handle a gun."

"Lucy, I am twenty-six."

"What did you say?"

"And I never knowed a girl like you before. All the girls I knowed was dirty and cussed and they didn't give a stomp how ignorant and low down I was."

"Ryder, why are you telling me this now? There's no time, man! We are in a terrible predicament and it's going to explode any minute! I am glad you figured out that you are only twenty-six, and it's good that you have found out that there are nice girls like me, but for the love of the Lord, man, let us go!"

"All right, all right," said Ryder, and took his second pistol from his holster and snatched up the lantern. "Give me your rock and let me chunk it at the door, and you let me do the talking. You stay behind me. If they wing me or kill me, don't hang around. Run. Save yourself. You hear me, Lucy?"

I did not answer. We left the trees and went back through the clearing. Ryder stopped for a second to douse the light in our lantern. We approached the shack in silence. When we were within about fifteen or twenty feet of it, Ryder changed his mind about his order for me to stay behind him and motioned me to position myself off to one side. I had never witnessed a cooler head. My own behavior was an argument. I felt that I was in a play and that in a minute the other performers would appear. I knew the danger and yet I stood there calm of heart holding my cocked pistol out before me with both hands. I heard the soft slap, slap of the river as it nudged its bank.

I saw Ryder draw his arm back and heard the thud of our rock as it hit the shanty door. Ryder shouted his order. "You in there! Your game is over! You done lost it. Let me see both of you come out that door now with your hands empty and up!"

Immediately the lights inside the shack disappeared. The door remained closed, but through its thin fabric there came the voice of Orlie. "Friend, I don't know what game you are talking about and why should we come out there with our hands up and empty? Who are you?"

"I am a deputy of the citizen's law and order and I am here to carry out my oath!"

"And your oath says you got to go around throwing rocks at the doors of innocent people? Well, I *will* be blamed. Here I thought I had heard of everything, but now you have told me something new. How much does this rock-throwing job of yours pay, deputy? If there is another opening on your force, I might be interested in it."

"Don't you play me for the fool," hollered Ryder. "I know who you are and I know you are holding Doctor Lyman Commander prisoner in there! Now do as I say if you want to live to see daylight tomorrow. Come out with your hands up and empty!"

"Friend, we don't have no doctor in here. I wished we did have because you sound like you need one. I think you need a head doctor. Where's the gal? I can't see her."

"Because she's gone. I sent her home."

"That's good. I hope she makes it. We been worried about her all day. Her horse throwed her and, when we found her, she couldn't say who she was or where she was from. You sweet on her?"

"I am sweet on getting this job done and am not going to fool around with it much longer."

"Friend, you hadn't got a job here. This here is a fish camp and my buddy and me own it, but it is closed now so you are trespassing. If you can read, you should've seen our signs on the way in. Chew on that for a minute. If you don't like the taste of it, let me know and maybe I can do something about it."

Ryder took a step forward. He was a real technician. His bullet left his gun and hit the door smack in its center, splintering it. "Boys, that is just a sample! I hadn't even started to get down to business yet! You ought to know I got the Chief out here with me, and he has deputized me to tell you if you come out one at a time with your hands up and empty there won't be no bloodshed!"

There was movement and noise inside the shack, and then Orlie's voice again. "If the Chief is out there with you, why ain't he the one doing the talking?"

I dropped to the ground and slithered over to Ryder grabbing him by his coat hem. "I forgot to tell you there is a window in the back room where they are holding Lyman.

108

It's been boarded over, but do you hear what I hear? No, wait. It's stopped now, but I know I heard it. You keep Orlie occupied. I am going to run around and see if something isn't going on back there."

"You will stay here!" said Ryder. "Get back over there and don't move. And draw your hood over your hair."

"I say," bawled Orlie, "if the Chief is out there with you, why ain't he the one doing the talking?"

Ryder stood steady. "He don't like to talk. He would rather act. You coming out?"

"No! I promised my mother I'd be home for my birthday, and that's day after tomorrow. She always bakes me a big cake with lots of goo on top, and I don't want to miss out on it. You and the Chief want to talk, go ahead and talk. I'll listen. But I don't want to hear that popgun of yours again. You have ruint my door. You pop it again and you will have to climb one of them trees back there for the top of your head. What say you now?"

"I say I don't want to kill you, but I will if I have to! The Chief and I are here to get the doctor and we mean to have him, and have him now! Send him out by hisself if you are ascairt of my popgun. We'll take it that way if that is the only way you will have it."

The equal to what happened next I hope I shall never hear or see again. There was a sudden commotion at the back of the shanty, and from around the corner of it there came Penn. He was aboard his horse and was riding it hard, kicking it with his feet and beating it with a length of board. There must have been nails in the board, for the poor beast screamed and lunged first this way and that. Seated behind Penn, roped to him at the waist and with his bound hands pulled around in front of the hoodlum, was Lyman. The panicked horse leaped through mud and pounded across rock. It shot past me and, in the moonlight, I saw its bared teeth. I was on the ground with my coat hood drawn down over my hair.

Ryder had sized up the situation quickly, but not accurately. His pistol was back in its holster, and he had taken his rifle from his shoulder and was aiming its barrel at the fleeing horse. He would have fired had I not done some fast thinking. "Don't shoot! He has Lyman! Didn't you see?"

"Great day in the morning!" exclaimed Ryder. For a moment both of us were inactive, and it was during this little respite that Orlie seized opportunity. From the shanty there came his high, gleeful howl. I did not hear his gunshot but I heard Ryder say, "Uh!" And then I saw him topple.

I was sure he was either dead or dying and leaped to him. He said, "Get down! Down, I say!" And I threw myself on the ground beside him. He flopped an arm over me, and I smelled the stench of his well-seasoned coat, and I thought, If we get back home, I am going to do something about that stink. My head was aching and my side was hurting. The sounds of Penn's departure had died away. I was not afraid, nor was I unafraid. There was a single star hanging south of the moon and I wondered at its brilliance.

And then from the back of the shanty there came Orlie

at full gallop astride his mount. He did not turn toward us, did not waste even one look in our direction, but headed straight into the woods.

"Don't move," cautioned Ryder. "It could be a trick. He might come back. Play dead for a minute."

I said, "Where are you hurt?"

"He got my leg," answered Ryder. The moon and stars had taken cover and the wind was up, clamoring at coming event.

In the shack we examined Ryder's wound. At his direction I poured kerosene from one of the lanterns into it and over it, and then we tore the tail from his shirt, pulled the damaged flesh across the injury, and bandaged it. After that was done I went, against Ryder's wishes, and brought the mule and Mary and Doctor's horse up to the shack. I left the buggy in the woods. A sack tied around the mule's neck contained food for both the animals and for us. Said Ryder, "I told you I was a man who always looked ahead."

"Congratulations. What are you doing?"

"I am dividing up these blankets one of them buckaroos forgot. We are going to sleep. You can drag the cot out here and we won't argue over which will spend the night on it. I'll bed down over there in the corner."

"Sleep! We are going to sleep while my brother is out there having only God knows what being done to him?"

"Chief, we cannot travel in the dark."

"Clegg's men aren't having any trouble with the dark."

"You're still on that, eh?"

"Of course. They are Clegg's men."

111

"You don't know that."

"Don't tell me what I know. It's not hard for me to add."

"Add what?"

"This afternoon that man who calls himself Orlie told me to watch my pride. He said if I didn't, I might see it in the dust."

"What's that mean?"

"It's one of Tom Clegg's expressions."

"And that's your evidence?"

"Listen, Ryder, and understand. Tom Clegg killed Papa."

"No, he didn't. A yearling did."

"Clegg was there. He kept Marion from going to Papa's aid."

"Why?"

"Ryder, I don't know. One time when both of them were young, Clegg wanted to marry Mama. Instead she married Papa because, don't you see, he was different from Tom Clegg. Papa liked muskrats and pigeons and icicles. You don't see, do you?"

"Lucy, girl," said Ryder.

"Oh, hush! I don't care whether or not you see. I see, and that's enough."

"It's raining," said Ryder, "and it's dark out there. There isn't anything more we can do tonight. Lay down. Quit talking. Don't think. Sleep. Are you warm enough?"

"I am all right. I will say I am not used to sleeping with all my clothes on. What about your leg?"

"It feels like it's been shot. Tomorrow morning when we light out from here we won't take the mule. We will leave it and come back for it and the buggy later."

"I thought you wanted to sleep."

"I can't. My mind won't shut up."

"Do you think Clegg's men will double back trying to fool us?"

"No. They've gone. They are smart, but I will have to side with you. I think they are working by orders and their orders has petered out. We messed them up. So, I am thinking if I was them I would head downriver and set up headquarters. Then I would sneak back to where my first orders came from and get me a new set. People like them two only go by orders because that is where their money comes from."

"I keep wondering how they could have known I would leave Jewel Sink this morning and ride in this direction."

With a grunt, Ryder rose from his blanket and limped over to the pile of Orlie's gear and fished out a spyglass. He said, "In their hurry to get out of here they forgot this, too. This morning when they nabbed you it wasn't any accident. Probably they had been watching Jewel Sink for days."

I said, "Blow out that light." And pulled my odorous blanket up around my shoulders.

Time was against us. I knew that and thought I would not be able to sleep, but presently my eyes could remain open no longer. The window in the little back room was now unhindered of its former barricades, and several times during the night Ryder got up and went to it and looked out.

Chapter Seven

Morning came with a soggy and irritable eye. The air was heavy, and out over the hills to our west there was pasted a spread of serious appearing clouds.

We did not get the early start I had hoped for. There were the horses and mule to be fed from the supply of grain Ryder had had the foresight to bring along, and when they had finished their meal I led them, one by one, down to the edge of the river to drink. Then, because the mule would have to forage for himself until we came back for him, I turned him loose.

The kerosene had not done much toward improving Ryder's wound. It was oozing and, when we removed the piece of shirttail so that we could look at it, it opened. Ryder did not want me to fool with it. I told him to hush and made another trip to the river, returning with a pail of fresh water. The pail was one of Slouch Hat's relics. It almost did away with our fire because it leaked, so Ryder carried it outside and sloshed the unheated water from it over his injury. I removed one of my stockings and we used that for a fresh bandage.

For our breakfast we shared a tin of canned meat and a box of soda crackers. Ryder used his pocket knife to open the tin and we scooped the meat from it with our fingers.

Ryder then checked his rifle and both pistols. He conceded to my argument that I should carry one of the weapons yet, when he handed me the smallest, he said, "Now all you need is a lipful of snuff and somebody to teach you some cuss words."

I said, "Ryder, I didn't make any of this. What would you have me do? Stay here and mind the hearth while you go after the bear that ate Junior?"

"You got a smart mouth on you," said Ryder. "When I first met you I thought you had one of the sweetest voices I had ever heard, but I've since changed my mind. Is your coat still wet?"

"Of course, but there's nothing to be done about it. I didn't think to bring an extra one with me."

We had a stern morning. Off and on it rained. We rode with all senses alert. About two miles east of the fish camp we picked up telltale signs of the trail we sought: hoofprints in wet, barren soil, a tossed whiskey bottle, an empty bean can. The can had been opened by some sharp-bladed utensil, and Ryder got down to examine it. We had turned away from the river.

The stop seemed an unnecessary one to me, and I said to Ryder, "We have their trail now so why are we standing here looking at their trash?"

"Chief," said Ryder, "I will be all right directly, but I got to rest for a minute."

"Rest! There's no time for rest!"

"I am feeling sickly," insisted Ryder, "and have got to

115

rest for a minute." He went to a tree and put his back to its trunk and lowered himself to the ground.

I got down and went to him and saw that there was a fresh stain on the leg of his trousers, the one covering his injury. "You're not a good clotter, are you?"

"I guess I'm not."

"Maybe there is something wrong with your blood."

"There is not anything wrong with it. It's red, same as yours."

"I think you had better stay here and I'll go on by myself. You are only hindering me."

"If you're tired of living, go ahead. I'll tell your mama you died brave. That will make her feel good."

"You leave Mama out of this. Do you feel weak?"

"No, I just like trees."

"You've lost that fat belly you used to have. You would have been better off keeping it. In an emergency people can draw on their fat."

"I didn't like it," said Ryder. "You mean this is the first time you've noticed it's gone?"

"No. I've been watching it, if you must have your vanity fed. Peel that mess off, and I'll give you my other stocking for a new bandage, and then maybe we can go on."

Ryder took his bottle of vanilla from his coat pocket and treated himself to a bracing draft. While I was removing my stocking he turned his head. The task of rebandaging his leg was not pleasant. We made a tourniquet with the stocking ends, tying them as tightly as we dared, and when this was done Ryder stood and took a couple of test steps,

116

but immediately had to return to his tree. His pain was humiliating to him and he was angry with it.

I was in a little difficulty myself. My broken rib reminded me not to cough or breathe too deeply. I thought to see it come poking through my skin at any moment, and I had my own anger, but I did not know what to do with it as I squatted beside Ryder. It seemed to me then that all the lives connected to mine were running to weak forms, that they had turned in the wrong direction to compete with me in some queer manner.

In that moment I could not see the use in the man before me. I only saw his weakness, and his weakness was exacting more of me and my predicament than I was willing to allow.

There was no time for tact, and so I said to Ryder, "Ryder, I don't like to leave you here like this but I must. I am going on without you."

Said Ryder, "Hooroar! No, you are not. You are going to sit right here side of me and wait. I will be all right in a minute."

"We don't have a minute. We have already wasted too many. Ryder, you are sick. You ought to see your face."

"And you ought to see yours. Them two customers we are after would like to see it on the end of a pole, and that's where they will put it be we not careful. They would like to make fish bait out of all of us. They are not suitcase farmers or anything like that. Be quiet. Sit still and let me catch my wind."

"Listen, I am going to my brother's aid if he is still

alive. If he isn't, if Clegg's men have killed him, I will feed *their* heads to the fish. Good-bye, Ryder. If Lyman and I don't make it back to Jewel Sink and you do, take care of Mama. Marion and Delia will help you. Tell Mama I said you are to have all my books. Don't feel guilty about this. It was never your fight. It's all Commander. I was wrong to drag you into this."

"If this fight is Commander, then it's Tuttle," asserted Ryder. "And the devil with your books! Do you think I would really want them if you wasn't there to explain them to me? Give me your hand. Help me up."

I said, "No. You're in no condition to go on." And jumped up and ran, not daring to look back even once for fear I would yield. I had Orlie's spyglass with me. Ignoring Ryder's shouted orders to "Come back! Wait, Lucy!", I boarded Mary, reined her around, and away we went, making our breakneck way through stem and tree and stalk. We were running in a southeastward direction and so was the wind.

We were in a kind of trough, and I was not sure of anything. From time to time we stopped and I used the spyglass to examine our all-around frame. Nothing human or belonging to human rewarded these inspections. Finally, in despair, I decided I had lost out.

It took Mary to show me that I was wrong. She was tired and would not be turned. She wanted water and, disregarding my proddings, trotted over to a little stream trickling down over some hill rocks. I dismounted and we took turns drinking, I from my cupped hands. The liquid was cold and flecked with silt. When I had had my fill, I walked away from Mary and stood in the center of our trough and again used my spyglass, training it first to my right and then to my left, making a slow and sweeping study. I listened to the silence in the magnitude all about. I was nowhere near to faith in my mission.

Mary had finished with her drinking and now was restless and excited. She pawed the ground and snorted, and came to me and put her head against my shoulder. I turned and it was then that I saw what I sought—a tree standing on a knoll at the turn of the walled-in gorge. It was south of my position and in its correct evergreen and shaped as it should have been, except there was something antic about its lower bole. Its layered, extended branches looked tied together as if someone had wanted to make of them a curtain. What I was observing was a hidey-hole, a clever and slapdash piece of engineering. At once I recognized it for what it was, and also at once I knew event was upon me.

Quickly, I took my place in it. There was no time for detailed planning. Mary was a concern. I knew I could not ride her down close to the site of the hideout, neither could I leave her there in the gorge for she would follow me and attract attention. So, in all haste, I took her reins in my hand and led her back up the ravine expecting with each step to feel a shot in my back. The climb to the overlooking woody ridge was a fairly formidable one, yet Mary followed me willingly; but when I found a safe and right place for her she balked at being picketed. I remembered the raisins and dried prunes and biscuit in her saddlebag, gave them to her, and left.

Using anything and everything offered in the way of cover, I ran back along the rim of the gorge to the point where Clegg's men had struck camp. Again looking down at it, it told me something I needed to know. At its back, one of the hoodlum's horses wandered, trailing its reins and nuzzling the earth.

I thought, So. I will only have to deal with one. The other has gone for new orders just as Ryder said he would. The little snub-nosed weapon in my coat pocket was cold reassurance. I rolled my spyglass up in one of the tailends of my coat and held it there. I wondered if the gun would accidently discharge if I should fall during the descent I intended to make.

It did not. Crouched low, my hood drawn over my head and as much of my face as it would cover, I left the ridge, jumping and twisting and turning, gathering momentum as I went. My aim was to wind up within the protection of a grass and bush grove on the ravine floor, and I did not miss it by far.

On my stomach I inched forward and used the spyglass. Dried weed clusters poked at me. I could not distinguish any movement from within the hideout. The loose horse had moved around to its front and continued to graze, but then it lifted its head as if sensing something bodeful. I laid the spyglass on the ground and took the gun from my pocket, gripping it with both hands and waited, for what I did not know. I only knew something had to happen.

A wash of air moved my bushes and grasses. Behind me and on both sides of me there was the great and candid decency of the unpeopled. I watched the hideout. There was a disturbance at one of its sides, and then out stepped Penn. He had been at too much of the "tangle-leg," was half drunk. He was armed. He came around the tree's front and, in the manner of a regimented schoolboy, exercised his arms and legs. He kicked at the ground and talked to the sky. Grinning, nonchalant, he moved toward me. I did not dare move. When he was within about ten feet from me, the outlaw stopped and leaned forward from his waist, peering. He sang out, "Hey, little red coat. Oh, little red coat. I see you in there."

I stood up and Penn took another couple of steps toward me. "Well now," he said. "I didn't think you was the type to ride off and strand your brother, but I will say I did not expect to see you show up here by yourself. That is plumb foolish. Now you have got it worked around to where I have got to be boss again."

I said, "You are not the boss of anybody, not even yourself."

"To you I don't look like I'm boss of myself?"

"To me you look like stable dirt. You are one of Tom Clegg's men and don't dare to spit without his say-so. I have come for my brother. If you are smart, you will consider your position. The deputy and the Chief from Church Falls will be here in not less than five minutes. They have your partner and he is more dead than alive, they have seen to that. If you don't want to wind up in the same condition, you will do as I say. Give up before they get here. If you do, I will put in a good word for you. If you do not, you will be taken back to Church Falls a corpse. You are mistaken if you think you are boss now. I showed you once I was not afraid of you and I will show you again. My brother is worth a hundred times the likes of you. If you would force me to kill you in order to save him, I will. Now which way is it to be? Yours or mine?"

Penn's answer was to raise his weapon and send a shot whistling past me. It happened fast and put a roar in my head. I jumped backward and fell into a bush and, for a moment, was involved in a tussle with its spiney arms. I heard Penn's laughter and the roar in my ears grew.

The roar was not in my ears! It was coming from some outside source. I raised up and looked at Penn and saw that he was hearing it, too. He stood with his mouth open and his eyes starting.

I twisted around and saw two things. Number one was Ryder. He was on Doctor Porter's horse and came slashing his way down the canyon yelling things I could not understand. Behind him there came rolling an earth-colored cloud, followed by a hissing, foaming, buckling water flood.

I saw Penn running toward the tree hideout, and I saw Lyman with a blanket wrapped around him, standing in what served as its doorway.

Ryder went past me, wheeled, and came swinging back. By this time I was free of the bush and was standing. Ryder snatched me up as if I weighed nothing. All in an instant I was on the horse with him, behind him, riding bareback, my arms wrapped around his middle. I screamed "Ryder! Lyman's in the tree! Look! The tree! Save him!"

"Hang on!" roared Ryder and spun his horse again, and we shot away to the tree. Ryder had a rope in his hands, and I saw it leave them as if it were alive and streak through the air and settle around Lyman's waist.

Again I screamed, "You can't drag him! You will kill him!"

If Ryder made an answer to that I did not hear it. He kicked the horse hard and away we went, Lyman being dragged and pulled and rolled. Manacled though his hands and feet were, he had managed to pull the blanket up around his face and his knees to his chest. Ryder had wrapped his end of the rope around the horn of the horse's saddle and was lashing the heaving, straining animal with his reins and kicking its flanks with his heels. And in this brutal and relentless manner we made our escape to high, safe ground with only seconds to spare.

Down the valley there came pouring a wall of water with all the speed of a crack train, violating everything in its path. It boiled in its center and its waves slapped the sides of the ravine. Its first wave was followed by a second and yet a third. The whole incident was finished in less than thirty minutes. Ryder and I could not give full and immediate attention to all it had wrought. There was my poor brother, savagely battered and unconscious, to be seen about first.

"He is dead," I said, looking down at him. "Oh, Ryder, he is dead."

Ryder was on the ground beside Lyman. He held his hand on Lyman's throat and then held it over his half-open mouth. "No. There's still some breath in him. Give me your coat."

We spread my coat on the ground and rolled Lyman from his blanket, which was badly torn, over on to it, and then Ryder covered him with his own coat. There was nothing we could do for him; we had no aids, and so we sat there, one on either side of him, and waited.

Lyman had taken a terrible beating. I watched blood from his cuts stain my coat, and I wondered how long it would be before it stopped. I tried to remember how it had been during the old good days when Papa was alive and life was complete in the elegant house at Church Falls.

I was holding one of Lyman's hands in mine and it was cold, without life, but then its fingers curved around mine in a weak protest. I looked down into the punished face and saw the eyes, so like Mama's, open.

Said the voice of my physician, "That was some ride you two gave me. Don't let how I look and act now scare you. And don't try to move me just yet. Keep me covered and let me rest a while."

I said, "Oh, Lyman, do you remember that time I ate

that whole chocolate pie, and Mama wanted to know which one of us did it, and I said it was you? It was for company supper and Delia didn't have time to make another. I'm so sorry, so sorry."

Lyman took no note of this silly confession. He moistened his lips with his tongue. "Tom Clegg," he said.

I bent to him. "What? Lyman? Lyman, talk to me. You said Tom Clegg. What about him?"

"Penn and Orlie are his boys."

"Did they tell you that?"

"No."

"They how do you know it?"

"Last night they had an argument."

"About what?"

"About who is boss. Orlie said Penn wasn't. He said Tom Clegg was."

"I knew it! I knew it all along. Lyman, look at me. *Look at me*. Is that all they said about Tom Clegg during their argument?"

"It's all I can remember."

"Where is Orlie now?"

"I don't know. Gone to Church Falls."

I asked, "How long ago did he leave?"

But Lyman had grown quiet. He was either unconscious again or was sleeping.

Ryder lifted a corner of the coat covering our patient and after a scrutiny said, "Chief, he is in bad shape and I don't know how we are going to get him home without making things worse. I would say I would take one of the horses and go after the buggy, but that would leave you here alone and Orlie might come while I am gone."

I said, "I will go after the buggy."

"No you won't either, and this time you will mind me. I am thinking if we could find us a couple of tree poles we could make us a drag."

"What is a drag?"

"It's a frame for hauling something you want to get from one place to another. If we can find us a couple of tree poles we can thread them through the arms of these coats and lay Lyman on them and then, if we don't go too fast and pick our way careful, that should do it I think. I am going to take off my underwear now and put your brother in it. It's long-handled and flannel and will help keep him warm. I see he is a good clotter. Did you lose my pistol?"

"I guess I did. I am sorry. I will buy you a new one if ever I see any money again. I told you Tom Clegg was behind this. Didn't I tell you?"

"Yes," said Ryder, "you did. But we hadn't got time to study on that now. Did you see which way Penn went when the water hit?"

"The last time I saw him he was running toward the hideout."

Ryder was preparing to undress. "I don't want you to see me naked. Take a little walk, but don't go too far. Penn might be up here with us somewheres. Take my pistol with you. Are you cold? If you are, I will give you my shirt."

I said, "I am fine." I was not but I said that and, while

Ryder started the job of divesting himself of his underwear, I walked to the rim of the ridge and looked first across to the matching summit to where Penn's horse wandered. He was looking for food and, as I watched, he lowered his head to a clump.

Now the sky was unmarred and there was light in the washed and plundered gorge. I looked down and saw at the turn of it the tree, which had served as hideout to Penn and Orlie, standing yet on its knoll. Its branches were muddied and swept back with the weight of mud, and among them, locked in them, was the body of Penn. His feet dangled and his arms were outspread, crucifixion style.

I left the ridge and went down to get a closer look at him. The light fell slantwise across his face showing me his last expression, outraged and perplexed.

Chapter Eight

Ryder looked only once at the body of Penn hanging in the tree in the gorge. He looked long and silently, and hugged his chest with his arms, and when he turned away I said, "Well, it isn't anything to regret! I don't see how you can feel anything for him. If I had time and the strength, I would go down there and shake him loose and throw him on the louse pile where he belongs."

"He was a human," said Ryder.

I said, "So was Papa. So are we all. Are you forgetting that?" I could not rouse him to the quarrel I wanted. He said, "Come away," and held out his hand as he would to a child, but I would not take it.

We were still on the ridge, but now we moved back to take cover among the trees. Our determination was to take a different course back to Jewel Sink than the one used by Orlie and Penn when they had entered the hills with me the day before, thus attempting a possible avoidance of a meeting with Orlie. The spyglass was gone, so we had to depend on our naked eyes in our watch for him. Ryder's horse was travel-jaded and Mary, now provided with companionship of her own kind, was content to stand drowsing.

The flood had not shocked her. She could not know how temporary and flimsy was our security there in the old biota. For her, the day's slate was clean. The air was becalmed and cold to the point of discomfort.

Construction of the rig on which Lyman would lie during the travel back to Jewel Sink was more of an undertaking than Ryder would admit, even as he hobbled around through the wilderness of oak and hickory with me, combing the forest understory to find two matching tree poles. And then, with only his pocket knife for a tool, he panted and tugged to strip them of their dead, stubborn limbs, and then panted and tugged more to thread them through the arms of the coats. The light on the horizon's bound was well past its mid-afternoon stage before we finished the job, and Ryder was having some trouble keeping his groans to himself. I asked him if his leg hurt him, and he said, "Never mind my leg."

Drifting in and out of sleep, covered with the torn blanket, Lyman lay on the ground nearby. He set his teeth when we lifted him and placed him on his travel bed. I pulled the pieces of the blanket up around him. Ryder then brought the horses from the trees, cut his lariat rope into two even lengths, and attached the bed's trailing poles to his horse's saddle.

Lyman stirred. Even his eyes were sapped of their color. He thought I was Mama and asked for a drink of water.

Preparing to mount, Ryder had laid his rifle across his saddle's pommel and had checked the pistol in his belt. He was patient. He fished an empty bean can from his saddlebag and handed it to me. "Go see can you find him some water, but be quick as you can about it. The daylight is not going to wait on us. I sure would hate to meet up with Orlie out here come dark."

Can in hand, I went down into the gorge searching for the place where Mary and I had drunk before the flash flood. I found the spot, but now the rivulets seeping down across torn earth and dislodged root and rock were so clouded with filth that, after I had filled my can, I could not see the bottom of it. I did not think I would find any better anywhere in the ravine, so again I climbed the cliff and ran along its edge hoping to find a source, a little spring or an unmuddied pool.

My hurried exploring brought me more, much more, than the water I had hoped to locate. It took me to the highest point of the cliff, to a spot opening out onto a wide rock slab, which was thick and covered with thin sod. Water, pushing up through natural plumbing from some nearby underground system slid around the edges of the rock slab and joined forces at its sharp free point, which struck out about a foot into space.

I went across the slab and lay on my stomach and held my can under the trickle to fill it. This process would not be hurried yet, hoping to hurry it, I inched forward. So did the shelf, ever so slightly. The movement was cause for a little alarm, yet I continued to lie there watching my can slowly fill. The wind passing through the trees made them creak and sway, and I looked down and out and saw a dark upright shape moving toward my bluff.

It was Orlie! He wore a wide-brimmed hat so I could not see his face, but I knew that figure. It was he all right. He did not look up, and in a minute was lost to my view. I kept waiting for him to reappear, but he did not. It took me a couple of seconds to figure out where he had gone. I was on the roof of a cave and Orlie was in it!

Holding my filled can, I stood up and took a step sideways. The balanced and tipped rock shelf stayed where it was. I took two more steps, backward this time, into stiff, arched grasses and forest duff. I set the can of water on the ground. My injured rib jabbed at my side. I was afraid I would cough. In my mind a dangerous plan was forming. How wide was the cave opening? Would the rock slab cover it? Why was I so sure that there was a cave beneath me? I wasn't. It was only a surmisal. I had to see.

On my hands and knees I went forward again, this time steering clear of the dislodged shelf. At the edge of my bluff I felt a rise of cold air, colder than the temperature around me. There was a hole in the side of the mound beneath me. When I pushed my head out and looked down, I could see it.

And I saw something else—Orlie's booted feet, the toes of them sticking up. The outlaw was inside the cave taking a ground rest. The feet played a little contented game with each other. Every minute or so they would disappear, and then out from the mouth of the cave would come sailing a bone. The outlaw was having a cold, early supper.

I went backward again into the grasses. I smelled leaf rot and was swept with a renewed sense of loss. I gazed at the rock slab, mentally sizing it, and wondered if my weight on its tip would cause it to fall straight down or if it would go sailing off into space, carrying me with it.

I found out. With a great crash it went straight down, landing upright and embedded against the cave opening, covering it all except an inch or two at its top. I was thrown clear and slid ten feet or so, grabbing at every limb and bush on the way.

When I stopped and was able to focus my eyes and stand, Orlie's shrieks assaulted my ears. "Hey! Hey, anybody out there? Hey! If there is anybody out there, make me know it! I am trapped in here! I am behind this rock and can't budge it!"

I watched a clan of birds come streaking from a thicket and disappear into the indifferent silence, and after a while the screaming from the cave stopped.

On my way back to the site where I had left Ryder and Lyman, I forced my heart and face to composure. Ryder wanted to know what had taken me so long, and I told him, "I took a bath. There was no sense in letting all that water back there go to waste." I knelt and held the can of water to Lyman's lips, and he drank until the can was empty, and then we started home. The *travois* performed better than either Ryder or I had expected it would. Some of the time I walked beside it, keeping an eye on Lyman.

We made it out of the hills before dark and then the moon came to make its contribution. Ryder, observing the cleared sky, called out, saying, "Well, I guess Old Master is through rolling his punkins under the bed for awhile. How are you and our patient making it back there, Chief?"

I answered, "Oh, we are making it, but I think we had better stop soon and rest. Have we any food?"

"We have grain for the horses and there is one can of meat left for us," replied Ryder. "Don't let your mind dwell on how empty your stomach is. Soon as we get home, Delia will fill it up for you."

I said, "I don't like this dark and think we had better not plan on seeing home tonight. We still have miles to go and I don't like to take unnecessary chances. You said yourself that horses can't see any better in the dark than we."

Ryder brought his horse to a stop, dismounted, and came back to Lyman and me. He knelt beside the drag to place his hand on Lyman's forehead. Lyman stirred and asked, "What's wrong? Why are we stopping?"

"We are just resting for a minute," explained Ryder. "Lay quiet. Don't try to talk. We'll have you home before sunup." He drew me away from the drag and we made some plans. Said Ryder, "We got to go on, dark or no. You ride my horse, and I'll walk ahead and be lookout for holes and such."

133

I said, "You can't walk all the way back to Jewel Sink. How do you think you could manage that with your leg the way it is? No, we will go on, but I will walk ahead and act as lookout for holes and such. You may keep Mary beside you. I've changed my mind about being hungry. That canned meat of yours tastes like tin. A little fire would be comforting. I don't suppose you have any matches."

"If they will still strike, I do have," said Ryder, "but we can't have a fire out here."

"Why can't we?"

"Have you forgot Orlie?"

"No."

"Then you have forgot how to think. If we built a fire and he is anywheres around, he would see it. I am not up to any more rescue work today, Chief."

"Nor am I. I wonder if my hair has turned white."

"So far as I can see it hasn't."

"You don't need to worry about Orlie anymore tonight, Ryder. He's back there."

"How's that again, Chief?"

"I said Orlie is back there. In a cave."

"You saw him?"

"When I went to get the water for Lyman."

"What was he doing?"

"Eating. Resting."

"Did he see you?"

"Not unless he could see through a slab of solid rock about a foot thick, and I don't think he could."

134

"Where was this slab?"

"At first it was on the cliff where I was getting the water for Lyman, but then I made it go over. Now it is covering the mouth of the cave where Orlie is. All except about two inches."

"How did you make it go over?"

"I ran and jumped on the end of it. It was ready to fall anyway, I suppose because of all the rains we've had."

Ryder walked around me twice. Far off, on the plains between the hills and home, the traveling moon laid its clear and honest light, and presently Ryder said, "I worked in a insane asylum one time."

"I have never seen an insane person."

"Usually you can't tell they are that way just by looking at them. You got to be around them a while first before you begin to take notice they are different. You still want a fire?"

"Maybe not. I don't think we could find anything out here to burn. Everything is damp and I'm not so cold as I was a minute ago. Look at the stars."

"Pretty."

"Should I feed the horses?"

"They would be proud if you did."

"Want me to open your can of meat for you?"

"No, thanks. My appetite has forgot me."

"We are supposed to be resting. Why don't you sit down?"

"I don't know."

135

"Do you feel all right?"

"I am better all over more than anywheres else."

"Want a drink of vanilla?"

"No, I can pass that up, too."

"What did you do when you worked at that insane asylum?"

"Stoked furnaces and scrubbed floors."

"Was that hard?"

"Then I thought it was. I worked from can till can't every day except Sunday. On Sunday I got to take some of the prisoners to church. Them that wasn't dangerous."

"You mean inmates."

"Chief," commented Ryder, "you got your English and I got mine."

"When we lived at Church Falls, Papa used to sing in the choir of the church we attended. He had a good tenor voice. He used to sing for our company when they came. Sometimes the songs he sang would make the ladies cry, and then he would switch off to a merry one and make them laugh. Tom Clegg was his friend then or pretended to be. He used to come to our house for dinner as often as Mama or Papa would invite him, but he cared nothing for the music afterward. One time he brought his son. Two peas in a pod."

"Chief," said Ryder, "we are going to let the law deal with Mr. Tom Clegg."

"Is that so?"

"Yes, that's so."

"And what about Orlie?"

"Him, too."

"He is clever and he is no weakling. I don't think he will stay in the cave back there long. I wouldn't if I were in his place. I'd figure a way out."

"Sure you would," said Ryder. "Knowing you I'd bet on it. But think about this. If Orlie gets away, and I say *if* he gets away, he'll be hunted for the rest of his natural life. He won't be able to trust nobody. He'll have to sleep with a gun under his pillow and every time he gets ready to go around a corner he'll wonder if it'll be his last. Now do you think he will like living like that?"

I said, "No. I wouldn't." The prairie before us was painted with moonlight.

So we went home, and Mama and Delia and Marion heard our story while they rushed to heat water for soothing baths, and applied healing ointments, and set before us bowls and mugs of steaming food and drink. Lyman was unable to sit at the table and feed himself, and Marion carried him to bed. Mama sat beside him hiding her own pain and the glitter in her eyes, and she spooned food into Lyman's mouth until he turned his head away, sighed, and slept.

The sun came, and in the old coigns Marion's pigeons gossiped. Delia built a fire under the laundry pot in the yard and into the soapy water stirred a pile of wash. I said to her, "After the blood and dirt have been boiled out of those, how about giving that coat of Ryder's a little sousing, too?"

She said, "You don't boil something that is part wool, Miss Biggety Brain."

"Then just wash it or fumigate it. Do something to it."

"Did Ryder tell you he wanted his coat washed or fumigated?"

"No, and I can't ask him. He's soaking his leg and doesn't want me to watch. It's a mess."

"You ought to try to sleep some."

"I had a little nap, all I wanted."

"Where'd you get that jacket?"

"It's Papa's. I like it because it has big pockets."

"What's the matter with your side?"

"Nothing. A little bruise."

Said Delia, "We are all a little bruised but, as soon as Ryder goes to Church Falls and makes his report to the sheriff, we'll feel better."

It was early March and now we were beginning to see and hear the annual renewal again, the greening, the warming stride each day a little nearer, the old perfection repeated. And soon would come the good summer, but this time different. Now, on shiny afternoons under the picnic trees, there would be one vacancy.

I asked Delia, "Where is Marion?"

"He's down in the west orchard taking out some of the trees."

"I think I'll ride down there and watch a while."

With her laundry stick Delia stirred the clothes sim-

138

mering in the washpot. "He left the lunch I made him on the table in the kitchen. Take it to him, will you? And tell him I said not to stay down there all day. Pulling stumps is mule work. They'll wait till we get the mule back."

The orchard where Marion worked, making the chips fly, digging into the rain-softened earth to loosen the ground binding the old stubborn roots, had paid toll to drought, disease, freeze, invading creepers, lightning strikes and the fires of hunters. Its will was gone. It was ready to die yet it continued to hug the earth.

I said to Marion, "I hate to see it go. I have always loved it in here. So did Papa. When I was a little girl and the weather was good Papa would bring all of us out here on Sunday afternoons and we'd plant things. One year we had so many tomatoes and strawberries and so much asparagus we didn't know what to do with it all. What we couldn't use Papa gave away to poor people. We took baskets and baskets of it back to town and went from house to house and everybody thought we were crazy. Papa made each of us put flowers in our hats or behind our ears."

Meditative, Marion leaned on his axe handle. "Your Papa was a cutup."

"Yes. Marion, it was all right for you to tell Ryder about what happened out at the Whidden farm the morning Papa was killed. It's good that he knows, but you haven't told Lyman or Mama, have you?"

Quiet and observant, Marion answered, "No, Miss

Lucy, and it won't ever get past me again. Delia either."

I handed him his lunch. "Mary and I are going to take a little ride. We are both restless."

"I don't wonder at that," remarked Marion. "Be careful where you go. Stay on our property."

There was nothing fateful in the orchard. The fateful was in Church Falls and it was locked behind a stone door in a cave in the hills.

Again Marion took up his axe and again the chips flew. For keepsakes I gathered a handful, storing them in one of my pockets. I would share them with Mama. She would like the feel and smell of them.

Mary and I left the orchard, dallying a little, playing the game, aware that Marion, between the swings of his axe, watched. But once the grove was behind us and the road to Church Falls was in front of us there was no need for pretense. Mary made her ears stand up. She had rested and was happy. Her belly was full and what was this? Another adventure?

Because it was too heavy for the weather I took Papa's jacket off but put it back on before we reached the town. Concealed in its right pocket was Ryder's loaded pistol.

It was a Wednesday and, traditionally, the merchants of Church Falls and their employees were taking a half-holiday.

Unseen, Mary and I clattered past the Packard Hotel. We went around it and entered the street where Tom Clegg maintained his plain offices. Through the stuff covering the windows of the front one I saw the moneylender at his desk. He was writing in one of his ledgers. When I entered his door he looked up and said, "Lucy." I don't have a name for what bubbled in his face. The other desk in the room was unoccupied.

I said, "Yes, it is I. No, don't stand. I don't want courtesy from you. We are beyond show now. We are beyond everything, you and I, and don't make the mistake of doubting me for an instant."

Clegg looked into the barrel of my pistol and swiveled his chair around, returning his pen to its inkholder.

In the act of removing the weapon from my pocket one of the wood chips had come with it, dropping to the floor. Clegg leaned, picked it up and placed it on the corner of his desk. He said, "What is that?"

I answered, "It's a wood chip from an apple tree. Have you never seen one? Have a good look at it. It's one of the last things you'll see."

Clegg lifted his head. He was breathing normally and, as if he saw in me some promise of release, some promise of deliverance known only to himself, his lips curled upward and in his gaze there was at once relief and a demand. His eyes were not those of a madman. They were intelligent and they yearned. They waited for my revenge, for me to return evil for evil.

There were footsteps in the street. Someone was passing, a man pushing a cart, whistling. He went on. I heard the creak, creak of the cart's wheels and the whistler's music fading and across the distance between Clegg and me, from his isolation, from his trivial realm and lack of innerness, something blew to me.

I felt the weight of the gun in my hand and my own isolation so close, bearing down on me, breathed its own demand. It was one of those times where decision controls all the years that will follow.

Chapter Nine

In Lyman's sleeping room at Doctor Porter's place I sat on the foot of my brother's bed and stroked its brass post.

Doctor Porter was absent. No one waited for him, no one came. The silence and my loneness was refuge, an undoubtful harbor, and presently I gave in and slept. Lyman's comforter over me was warm and light. I had not secured the door of the room for the key to its lock was missing, yet I slept. When I woke, I looked into two eyes. Those of a rattlesnake would have been friendlier. Said Ryder, "All right, Chief, just what do you think you're doing?"

I pushed the comforter back and sat up. "Do you have to talk so loud? I'm not deaf. Is there a fire in the house? A wolf at the door?"

Ryder was fussed and having some trouble with his speech. "Don't you sass-mouth me. I won't have it. I asked you what was the big idea and I want your answer."

I said, "I have been to settle things with Tom Clegg. I did and then I came here and went to sleep. I was tired. What time is it?"

"I don't know. What do you mean, you have been to settle things with Tom Clegg."

"They are settled."

"He's dead?" said Ryder, leaping to assumption. His eyes were shocked and bulging.

I said, "More than less, I think."

"Hooroar!" exclaimed Ryder, and made his breath whistle though his teeth. And then, as if from some distance, he asked, "Where's my pistol?"

"It's here. Somewhere."

"Give it to me quick."

"I can't find it. Oh, I remember. I put it over there on the chair. Ryder, what are you doing?"

Ryder had his coat open and was shoving the pistol into the belt strapped around his waist. That done he said, "Now. I am the one who killed Clegg, you understand? You didn't have nothing to do with it. Where was it you settled things with him?"

"In his office."

"Was he by hisself?"

"Yes."

"Did anybody notice you when you went to his office?"

"I don't think so. It's Wednesday. Everybody is having their usual half-holiday."

"Did you shoot Clegg in the head or where?"

"Ryder," I said, "I did not tell you that I shot Clegg. In my mind he is dead more than less, but I didn't touch him. I didn't even say much to him nor did he say much to me. You are always talking about destiny. Well, I stood there looking at him, and then I knew that killing Clegg wasn't mine. There was this man who went by outside pushing a cart and I dropped one of these wood chips on the floor and Clegg picked it up and asked me what it was and I told him. It was in that moment that I knew what wasn't mine to do. So far as I know Clegg is as alive as he ever was, which isn't saying much. Have you been to see the sheriff about Orlie?"

Ryder had tottered to a chair. He sent me a look. "I have. Why do you keep holding your side like that?"

"It hurts. I think I have a broken rib. What is the sheriff going to do about Orlie?"

"He's already doing it. Him and a deputy left for the hills about thirty minutes ago. I would have gone with them except I was too busy tracking you."

"They'll never find that cave."

"They'll find it. I drawed them a map. There aren't too many caves out there with rock doors on them."

"Did you tell the sheriff Orlie was working for Clegg when he and Penn kidnapped Lyman and me?"

"I told him. He said where was my proof, and I told him I didn't have any except what he'd find in the cave and Lyman's say-so. He said why would Clegg want to do you and Lyman harm and I had to tell him that it wasn't anything wrote out anywheres in black and white. He wasn't crazy about the job I handed him. I had to remind him that we are taxpayers and are the ones helping to pay his salary. Doc Porter was a help to me."

"Doctor Porter was present during your conference with the sheriff?"

"He was at the jailhouse seeing to one of the cell prisoners and when he heard all the commotion I was raising he came out and added his say to mine. If you ask me or even if you don't Lyman could do a lot worse than be hooked up with something like that old kick. There wasn't anything wrong with the boy he was at the jail tending to but homesick. He was bawling and Doc Porter sent to the Packard Hotel for him a good homecooked meal. Paid for it, too."

I said, "Ryder, did you or Doctor Porter give the sheriff a description of Orlie?"

"Doc Porter said he never actually saw Orlie's face," answered Ryder. "And neither did I if you'll think back. You and Lyman will have to be witness to him being one of your kidnappers when he is brought in."

"Will the sheriff and his deputy bring Penn back, too?"

"I guess they will. They can't leave him hanging out there in his tree. He'll get a John Doe funeral."

"Ryder," I said, "Let's not any of us who know ever tell Lyman or Mama how Tom Clegg kept Marion from going to Papa's aid the day he was killed. It would only hurt them more than they have been hurt."

Ample and clean was Ryder's expression then. His eyes were full. He went to one of the windows and raised it and stuck his head out of it. The clock in its tower in the town square was tolling the hour. I told Ryder that we should go home, that our family would be worried about us. He said we were waiting for Doctor Porter and went to Lyman's closet and gathered enough clothing for several changes.

Doctor Porter came and while Ryder waited in another room I was required to stand half naked and allow the cage that housed my ribs to be tightly wound round and round with long, wide strips of some stiff surgical material. Doctor Porter was almost sober. He advised me against doing any heavy lifting or engaging in any strenuous exercise until my broken bone had knitted. When the work on me was finished Ryder was called in to have his wound cleaned and dressed.

It was midmost afternoon before we got our start back to Jewel Sink. Ryder left Doctor Porter's horse with its owner, insisting that he could make the trip under his own steam. He and the doctor shook hands. "Tomorrow," promised Ryder, "I'll be going after our mule and I'll bring your buggy back, too." He declined my offer to let him ride Mary home. In the high manner of one who has found his destiny and found it to be good he strode alongside Mary and me. He walked straight and neither he nor I spoke of Tom Clegg or Orlie. Around the watered sloughs in the woods on both sides of us there were patchworks of tender green and the sky's day colors were draining away to the west. It was dusk before we turned into our lane and saw the lights of home.

We did not have word concerning Orlie until the next morning. The sheriff and his deputy came just after sunup and they had Penn draped across the rear of the deputy's horse. It fell to me to go out and officially identify the body. Lyman was sleeping, still recuperating.

It did not sicken me or frighten me to look at Penn. I said to the sheriff, "It is he."

The lawman turned to Ryder. "As you can see we didn't get the other one. By the time we located the right cave he had flown the coop."

"Are you sure you had the right coop?" asked Ryder.

"Oh," responded the sheriff, "it was the right one, no doubt about it. The rock slab you said this little lady here covered the opening with was laying flat on the ground outside it."

I said, "Did you see any chicken bones lying around?"

"Several," answered the sheriff.

I said, "Then you had the right cave. Before I pushed the slab over Orlie tossed some chicken bones out."

Mama, who was standing in the yard with the rest of us, looked once more at the body of Penn and said, "What a waste." She offered the peace officers breakfast but the sheriff said that they were in a hurry to get back to Church Falls. He asked me to furnish him with a description of Orlie and wrote it all down on a pad he took from his pocket.

We watched the officers mount up. Asked Ryder, "Then this is far as you're going to go with it?"

"It's as far as we can go," said the sheriff. "We'll take this one back to town and get him buried and we'll put a flier out on the other one. He might turn up in North Carolina or Tennessee or somewhere one of these days. If it happens somebody will let me know and then I'll let you know. But I wouldn't count on it. There's a lot of places for outlaws to hide. Meanwhile if I was you all I wouldn't go around accusing Tom Clegg of being mixed up in this. You've got no evidence you can back up, so it would be word against word and he might get you on a charge of defiling his character." He was fiddling with the brim of his hat. "If I was you all I'd take some extra precautions. Put some bars across the windows and some extra locks on the doors and don't go anywhere except in pairs."

There was a young wind blowing across Jewel Sink. It lifted the hem of Mama's short cape and for one moment I saw her, shaken and apprehensive, saw her acknowledge reality and bend to it. But then with a rebuking and angered motion she drew the cape around her and I saw the hardiness in her. She raised her hand to the sheriff and thanked him and we watched the two law officers ride from our yard.

Delia had our breakfast ready. We had stewed apricots, battered eggs and biscuits.

Epilogue

The days at Jewel Sink. Bold they were because, as with all people who know the ideas of rightness, who resist the opposite, who choose to be as whole as their natures will allow, we did not lock ourselves away into safe and comfortable shelter, there to live out our time free of peril and untouched by others.

There is no such thing as freedom from peril. Peril is faithful and unforeseeable and it is everywhere. It walks by night and walks by day and is no respecter of rules.

What we had at Jewel Sink talked back to our possible peril in simple language. There were the old orchards. We watched them, thinned and cleared of their dead, under new management, take hold and produce.

There was the mule in the fields. Ryder would not use a whip on him nor would Marion and so the animal went his own pace, and the sharpened blade of the plowshare bumping behind him dug into the useful land.

We made our peace. It came and stayed. And though in its beginning there were dark, private moments when I doubted the honor in this silent defender, by and by I found myself able to think of Tom Clegg as one recollects some fiendish childhood temptation. When wronged, the wild in the young know how to destruct. They know about the ways of injustice and they know about revenge.

I know about revenge. One day I held it in my hand, my finger on its pulse while the taste of its dreadful food filled my mouth. There was no fear for my personal safety, so I don't know what cause held me back. There was a denial of the kind that orders the intelligence in one person to be not overcome by the existence of evil in another. From where does a denial of this nature spring? I don't know. It has to be old, this instinct to let evil be its own slave.

About the Authors

With the publication of their first book, *Ellen Grae,* in 1967, Vera and Bill Cleaver created a sensation in the world of children's books. Since then they have broken all the rules, combining daring contemporary themes with the traditional values of humor, imagination, authenticity, and fine writing, and they have received outstanding critical acclaim. "That children's books are richer for the Cleavers there is no doubt," said *The New York Times Book Review* on publication of *Where the Lilies Bloom.*

Books by the Cleavers have been nominated four times for the distinguished National Book Award and have been included on such important lists as the American Library Association's "Notable Books," and *School Library Journal's* "Best Children's Books."

Vera Cleaver was born in South Dakota, Bill Cleaver in Seattle, Washington. They pursue their successful writing career, as well as their special interests in art, music, and nature, from their home in Winter Haven, Florida.